I0575312

BETRAYED
BY
LOVE & FAITH

A Journey Through Broken Trust

DR. MARCUS ANDERSON

Published by The Writehood LLC.

Paperback ISBN: 979-8-9945289-1-4

Library of Congress Control Number: 2026900871

To preserve confidentiality, certain names, locations, and dates have been modified.

Cover design: Generated with the assistance of artificial intelligence

Editor: Imani Williams-Sparks

For more information, visit the author's website:
www.thewritehood.com

DEDICATION

I dedicate this book to the resilient, to those who kept praying when answers did not come, who kept standing when their world was shaking, and who discovered that God's presence remains steady even when life is not. May you walk forward with courage, anchored in truth, unafraid of your story, and confident that healing is not only possible but promised.

Your future is not defined by what hurt you, but by the strength God is cultivating within you. Continue believing, continue growing, and continue becoming the person you were created to be.

ACKNOWLEDGMENTS

I give honor and thanks to God, whose grace sustained me through seasons that tested my strength and deepened my faith. This book exists because His presence never left me, even when the path was unclear.

To my children, thank you for being my constant source of motivation and hope. You remind me daily why perseverance, healing, and growth matter, and I strive to model a life of resilience and integrity for you.

I am deeply grateful for the friends and spiritual leaders who walked beside me during uncertain moments. Your wisdom, encouragement, and compassion helped steady me and reminded me that no journey is meant to be traveled alone.

To you, the reader, thank you for opening these pages. It is my sincere hope that within this story you find strength to move forward, courage to heal, and faith to believe that your past does not define your future.

This book is not only a reflection of what was endured, but a testament to what can be rebuilt. I move forward with gratitude, confident that even life's hardest chapters can lead to purpose, renewal, and greater becoming.

CONTENTS

INTRODUCTION

I did not set out to write this book. I wrote it because silence was no longer an option.

Betrayal has a way of dismantling life quietly at first. It does not arrive all at once. It enters through trust, through love, through faith, and then slowly unravels what once felt stable and certain. When betrayal comes from the people you are closest to, it fractures more than relationships. It fractures identity, belief, and the sense of safety you once carried without question. This book tells the story of that fracture.

I was a devoted husband, a father, and a man of faith who believed deeply in commitment, integrity, and doing what was right. I trusted the structures I had built my life around and the people within them. When betrayal entered my marriage, my family relationships, and my faith community, it did not simply break my heart. It disrupted my emotional stability, my mental clarity, and my spiritual foundation.

What followed was not just grief, but confusion. Anxiety that I could not easily explain. Intrusive thoughts that felt foreign and overwhelming. Moments of emotional collapse that forced me to confront how deeply betrayal can affect the mind and body. I learned that betrayal is not only a relational wound. It is a form of trauma.

This book is not written to assign blame or to relive pain for its own sake. It is written to tell the truth about what betrayal does to a person and what it takes to survive it. It is written for those who have felt isolated in their pain, questioned their worth, or wondered why they could not simply "move on."

Faith is an important part of this story, but it is not presented through easy answers or spiritual platitudes. My faith was tested, strained, and at times felt distant. I wrestled with questions I never expected to ask and discovered that faith, when honest, is not always neat or comforting. Sometimes it is quiet endurance. Sometimes it is choosing to keep going when clarity has not yet returned.

As you move through these pages, you will encounter moments of loss, disillusionment, and confrontation, but also moments of insight, resilience, and growth. Healing did not come quickly, and it did not come without cost. It required facing painful truths, seeking help, and learning to rebuild from the inside out.

If you are reading this because you have experienced betrayal in love, family, or faith, know that you are not alone. Your reactions make sense. Your pain is real. And healing, while difficult, is possible.

This book is an invitation to understand betrayal more clearly, to name what it takes from us, and to begin reclaiming what it does not get to keep.

PART I

THE LIFE WE BUILT

CHAPTER 1

OUR BEGINNING

O ur story didn't start with heartbreak. It started with hope. I remember the first time I saw Leslie and how her smile lit up the room like she was the main attraction. Her laugh made me feel like the most important person in the room. We were young, full of dreams and promises. Back then, love meant forever and that was worth protecting. I was a man who believed in commitment, loyalty, and doing what was right no matter what it cost me.

Leslie and I met in a way that felt almost scripted by fate. It wasn't flashy or dramatic, just two people crossing paths in a moment that would change everything.

I still remember the first time our eyes met and everything around me quieted around us. The way we looked at each other felt like a movie scene.

Her smile was warm and genuine, and something inside me told me this was the start of something rare. It reminded me of the time she sang at a convention when we were in high school. She sang, "The One I Gave My Heart To" by artist Aaliyah. We met in high school and her friend liked me, but I liked her. We talked on the phone for a little while during that time and remained cool with each other.

We ended up attending the same university. Leslie was one year older and a grade higher than me. When I arrived at college, she saw me and said "Oh my God, Terrance, you're going to school here? It is great to see you." We stayed in touch throughout the years but didn't date or anything.

Our early days were filled with discovery. We talked for hours, learning about each other's hopes, fears, and what made our hearts beat faster. She was different from anyone I'd ever known, kind, strong, with a spirit that radiated joy and conviction. We laughed over dates, shared dreams under starlit skies, and made promises without fully understanding the weight they carried.

From the beginning, our relationship was built on deep values. We believed in faith and honesty. We believed in a strong family. A home filled with love, a marriage that could withstand anything, and children who would grow up knowing the power of unconditional support. We committed not just to each other, but to the ideals we both held sacred, loyalty, respect, and the belief that together we could build something lasting.

Our courtship was simple yet profound. Every step forward felt like a brick in the foundation of the life we imagined. We believed in teamwork, in putting each other first, and in creating a legacy of love that would ripple through generations.

We started dating in college, closer to my graduation. I ended up graduating and moving to another state while we were dating. She moved in months later and was pregnant not too long after. I proposed while she was pregnant with our first child.

We went out on a date to a fancy restaurant, and I had the waiter bring out one rose at a time until he brought out the engagement ring that was in one of those butter containers. Leslie was so lost, she said why they keep bring me flowers. I said I do not know, you must have won something.

I opened the little fancy butter container and pulled out the engagement ring. I got on my knee and asked Leslie if she would marry me and want to spend the rest of her life with me. Leslie excited yell yes, crying with joy. She said I love you so much Terrance and I want to spend the rest of my life with you. This was one of the most beautifully aligned moments of my life and I was happy that the restaurant's workers were all in on it.

We were in love with each other so much that the world knew. Leslie planned the wedding; we got married out there and enjoyed every moment of it.

Leslie and I married with stars in our eyes, surrounded by family, friends, and the steady rhythm of faith that anchored us. It wasn't just the union of two people; it was the fusion of dreams, faith, and hopes with purpose.

We stood in front of loved ones, vowing to navigate life side by side. We vowed to be faithful to each other and be together till death do us part.

CHAPTER 2

BUILDING A FAMILY

W e built a family that looked just as strong on the outside as it felt like on the inside. Our home quickly filled with the joyous chaos of five children. Ilana, Darien, Lauren, Jaiden and Will. The soundtrack of laughter, scraped knees, bedtime stories, and Sunday mornings at church began. Their laughter echoed the halls, feet stomped across the floors, and voices filled every inch of our house.

Sundays felt our reset. Leslie and I would always be in a rush with seemingly millions of things to do before dinner. It was always best to prep things Sunday evening. Once we got home from brunch we started ironing clothes, figuring out the weeks hair styles, and making sure everyone had their shoes at the door. At the end of it all when it was time for dinner, I would look to Leslie proudly because I was happy to be building a life together that was bigger than what we imagined.

We built traditions, shared secrets, and dreamed together. We had our own inside jokes and familiar expressions. We laughed till our sides would hurt. Late night conversations in the dark were my favorite, especially when the house was silent. Some nights we stayed in the living room while the kids were in bed to enjoy each other's presence and the peace surrounding us. Those moments felt sacred to me.

The Beautiful Life We Built

We were what people called "The perfect family." And for a little while, it really felt that way. We weren't just a couple with kids. We were a unit, a team, a full-hearted family with laughter in our home and love in our routines.

We took pride in making memories together. Family trips were our tradition, each one carefully planned, full of excitement and wonder. I can still picture our kids packed into the van, fighting over the window seats, while my wife played the road-trip playlist we always listened to. Lauren brought the energy to the car ride while the boys crack jokes or pretended to be too grown for car games. Ilana was the loudest one most of the time. It was never a dull moment.

There were beach trips where we built sandcastles until sunset. We took mountain hikes with little legs slowing us down but hearts full of adventure. We did hotel stays where everyone piled into one bed for movies and snacks. I remember looking at Leslie and feeling like my life was full. My wife said, "Terrance, can you believe we have five little humans by us". I would say I know right and we just smiled and laughed.

One year, we took the kids to Disney World. I worked multiple jobs to make it happen, and the joy on their faces made every hour worth it. My wife and I held hands in line, watching our children laugh and scream on rides. Life always seems to feel like we did something right. I felt like I was giving my family the life I promised to give them.

Date nights were our reset button. Even with five kids, we carved out time just for us. We'd dress up and leave the chaos behind for a couple of hours. We would go to our favorite restaurant or lounge, nothing fancy, but it was ours. Leslie would order her usual, I'd try something new. Sometimes we'd talk about everything and nothing. Sometimes we just sat in silence, holding hands across the table. Other times we dance the night away. I had fun going out dancing and listening to music. We love live music as well. I felt proud to be hers.

Eating out as a family was always a scene, but a joyful one. Five kids talking at once, passing food, making a mess, and asking for dessert in the middle of the meal. People would stare at us like we were out of control, but I never cared because we were together. We had our "go-to" spots, pizza nights, Saturday morning pancakes, and special ice cream runs when someone did well in school. We created a family culture. Out family celebrated each other while at the same time being there for each other in the darkest hours.

At church, we were the picture of togetherness. We walked in all dressed up. The kids in a line like ducklings. Leslie by my side, hand in mine. People would smile at us and say, "You're so blessed." And we were. At least, that's how it felt.

Some nights we had spontaneous dance parties in the kitchen while cooking dinner. Leslie played music and everyone would wait for me to join in on the dancing. I'd pretend I didn't want to dance while still doing it anyway. We laughed a lot in those days, inside jokes and silly traditions. We had chore charts on the refrigerator, birthday parties in the backyard or at a venue, and game nights where no one played by the rules. When you think about it, it wasn't perfect, but it was beautiful. It was ours.

I hold own to these memories with love. Those memories were real, I was there, and I felt it. Nothing can erase what we once had.

Raising five kids is like beautiful chaos only experience can explain. From the moment our first child was born, our lives changed in ways I hadn't fully imagined. Even now, I think back to the moments of pure joy, the first smile, the first step, and the sound of their laughter echoing through the house. But alongside that was challenges that tested every ounce of patience and strength we could even have. Our days included a whirlwind of diaper changes, school runs, soccer games, and late-night talks. Each child was unique, with their own personality, needs, and dreams.

I remember one particular evening, the house buzzing with noise. Leslie and I were in the living room in our separate worlds as the kids fussed over toys and spilled juice. My wife and I exchanged a glance, exhausted but smiling, knowing this was the life we had chosen. She shouts for them to stop and the house becomes a bit quitter. Leslie laughed soft and so did I.

We couldn't help but find humor in the situation. Ilana came to tell us what happened but in the end they all went back to playing together. Despite the mess and madness, there was a deep sense of fulfillment. Our family was our greatest accomplishment.

"Terrance," Leslie said, "tell me this is normal." I thought about it for a moment before picking up a shoe to one of my daughter's toys. "If this is not normal, something is not right at all.", I responded.

Our children were always different from each other. They had their own personalities which meant there was never a dull moment. Jaiden was always trying to be a grown up, convincing himself that he didn't need help. He was always the one delegating. He was the oldest of the five. The other kids looked up to him. Will was the comedian. Anytime something was wrong he know how to lift everyone's spirits. He looked up to his older brother. They loved playing basketball with each other. Lauren was outspoken, quick witted, and loved to dance. Always marching to the beat of her own drum.

Darien is the Curious George of the family. There was never a moment where he wasn't talking. Darien was the type to follow you around the house asking questions and telling stories. If you let him, he'd follow you to the bathroom and talk from the other side of the door.

He was the fourth kid who gave me the time of my life when he was younger. On the other hand, Ilana was small and a little shy to outsiders but at home she was full of energy. The loudest one in the room sometimes. Our kids were and still are the most exciting parts of our relationship.

Faith played a central role in grounding and holding our family together. We believed that our family was a gift and a responsibility, a community within a community. Sundays were sacred time for church service, followed by lunch. Some Sundays we would go eat to a restaurant after church. Every Sunday morning, we did the same routines. I would get the kids clothes ready and Leslie fixed everyone's hair. The kids had the responsibility of hunting downing their shoes. I would rush everyone out of the house and into the van. I was always the driver.

Once we left the house it became an obstacle keeping everyone clean enough for lunch afterwards. Leslie would give them a full run down on how to stay clean. These moments gave us strength and connection. It was a reminder that we were part of something bigger than ourselves. Our faith wasn't just about rituals; it was woven into our daily lives. When we got to church people smiled, called us blessed. I smiled back in agreeance because I truly believe it.

We prayed together, celebrated milestones with gratitude, and taught our children to seek kindness and forgiveness. The values we held dear, love, honesty, and faithfulness were the pillars we hoped would carry them through life. Yet, the pressure to maintain appearances was real. We wanted others to see a strong, united family, even when exhaustion and stress threatened to pull us apart. There were times when we smiled through the disarray, not wanting to admit how hard it really was.

Building a family wasn't perfect; it was messy, complicated, and beautiful in its imperfection. Every late-night conversation, every bruised elbow, every shared prayer added layers to the story we were writing together. Those years taught me more about love, sacrifice, and resilience than anything else ever could.

Our family was a living testament to faith in action, a daily miracle of forgiveness, hope, and commitment.

CHAPTER 3

STRONG ON THE OUTSIDE, WEAK ON THE INSIDE

From the outside, we looked like the perfect family. The kind people admired. One with five kids, a loving husband and wife, who served at church and showed up proudly for the community. Neighbors would smile and say, "You guys have it all figured out." Friends complimented us on our "strong marriage" and well managed family. Social media pictures showed happy faces, family gatherings, trips, birthday parties, and milestones. I let everyone believe storyline I was curating because no one really questions social media.

But appearances are deceiving. The cracks started early, subtle but growing, like hairline fractures in what looked like solid glass.

Although the early years of our marriage didn't have a lot of major issues, the first concerning one started with one of our children and Leslie. All our children slept in the bed with us for a very long time. Night after night there was a baby in the middle, a toddler stretched out between us, and one of the older kids at the foot of the bed. I would always ask Leslie to put the child in the baby bed next to us since it was in the way of intimate time with my wife. She would tell me it was fine and go back to sleep.

One night, my oldest son was sleeping in the bed with us and what seemed like the worst thing ever happened. Somehow, he slipped from the bed onto the floor. We had a headboard and a little crack from the mattress from that headboard. My son fell through the small crack. I never saw it as dangerous until it happened. I still do not know how it was possible since the crack didn't seem that big and he didn't wake us up before falling through to the ground. When we heard the boom, we both jumped up, and we noticed he was not in the middle.

Leslie started screaming before I got up from the bed and flipped the bed up with all my strength. My heart started pounding as I was expecting the worse. Leslie grabbed my son and we both held him. Our son started crying immediately. I think he was more scared because we were, not because he was actually hurt.

The next day, I walked into the bathroom and froze from shock. Leslie was standing there holding a razor. At first, I couldn't process what happened and when I saw the marks, reality set in. My wife cutting herself with a razor. My voice was shaking with fear as I questioned what she was doing.

She looked at me with tears rolling down her face and said that what happened the night before was her fault. I told her it was an accident, our son is okay, do not do that to yourself. I embraced her with my strong arms, held her wrist, and reassured her that everything would be okay.

She began sobbing in a way that I had never seen before, almost like she was collapsing from the inside out.

After seeing her cut herself to inflict pain, I was very worried as to who this person is. I have never experienced someone harming themselves, and I had no idea what to do with fear that was suddenly placed inside of me. I prayed hard to God, as this concerned me. I kept wondering over the months why she would do this to herself. Why did it seem like something deeper was hiding under the surface?

We would travel out of state to visit family often. We took many trips as a family but equally as many as a couple. Knowing all of the great memories and laughed more than anything which is why the bathroom situation was so hard to understand. It didn't match the woman I thought I knew but it made me pay closer attention to her moving forward.

As time continued, there were things about Leslie that didn't go unnoticed. Her smile didn't go from ear to ear anymore. Her laughter came less often and many days she felt more distant. Seeing things change in her made me feel like maybe our home wasn't as happy as I thought. Maybe it wasn't as strong as I thought. I noticed she would speak to me in a loud negative tone.

One Wednesday after our church's youth night, we were standing out front in the courtyard. The kids were running around and playing around Leslie and me.

Darien and Ilana seemingly needed the most attention since they were clinging to us. One had my sleeve while the other was attached to Leslie's leg. Jaiden was always famous for going on a snack hunt while Will talked over everyone to tell on him. Even with the current chaos, Lauren was the cherry on top, continuously asking for things that I said no to.

On the way back home from church, the kids continued the chaos. I noticed that Leslie was disassociating from the environment. It wasn't hard to tell that something was wrong that she wasn't ready to share with me. She used to share everything right away no matter how difficult it was, now she leaves me in the dark. "You good?" I asked. "I'm fine," she said with no hesitation.

She seemed to use that phrase often. Even when things needed more than just those two words. Not to long after that car ride, real life started pressing in. It never showed up in the post I made but it made the things unspoken sound really loud. The first big burden happened when Leslie showed me that she was having a hard time keeping steady work.

Leslie came home one afternoon seemingly exhausted from her work day. I was in the kitchen at the time and she dropped all her things into one of the kitchen table chairs. "I've decided it's time to leave my job," she said. I turned around from the refrigerator with lunch meat and cheese in hand.

I couldn't believe my ears. I looked at her with confusion and said, "What do you mean?" "I resigned." She replied, as if it was a normal sentence. She claimed that she was being disrespected and her boss didn't like her. Nothing made sense to me.

When I realized she was serious I stopped what I was doing. The day was already off to a chaotic start and breakfast from that morning still needed to be cleaned up but I still remained calm. "So, what's the plan?" She shrugged, as if she didn't care that the responsibility was all on me until she found something else. My wife said she would find something else but struggled to hold a job.

A year after Leslie was working her career job, we were living in Alabama then, she resigned for personal reasons. Her career job put her as a no-rehire in the state. After I found that out, I wondered if she did something else because why would her supervisor put her as a no-rehire for the entire state.

Time and again, she would take a position only to leave after a few weeks or months, always blaming the manager, coworkers, or the unfair workplace. But over time, I began to see a pattern that no one else seemed willing to acknowledge. The problem wasn't with them; it was with her.

At first, I told myself it was temporary hardship. Maybe she was in the wrong place at the wrong time. Maybe she needed more support. I even tried to convince myself that the places she was working at are unfair. But the constant cycle wore on our family's finances and added tension I couldn't ignore. I tried to talk with her about it gently. Maybe there's something we can do to help, I'd say, "Have you thought about why these jobs aren't working out?" Her reasons changed over and over but my feelings remained the same. I was over it. Every time she quit, I worked more jobs exhausting myself.

However, I wanted to be the provider and make sure my wife and kids had everything they needed and many things they wanted.

One afternoon, Leslie came home from another interview with anger written all over her face. She looked like she was going through the argument she would've had with the person who interviewed her. "They just don't get me," she said, tossing her purse on the table. "It's like they were criticizing me before they even knew me," she said. I pulled a chair out and asked her to sit with me. "Share with me what happened?" She waved her hand indicating that she didn't get the job.

My wife told me that she didn't even know if she wanted the job. I figured that was her way of being a sore loser about the situation. She was always defensive, shifting blame. It was exhausting. I wanted to believe her, but inside, I felt like I was losing her piece by piece. After listening to her and trying to find the best way to be gentle, I simply said, "Maybe there's something I can do to help you." I looked at her resume and cover letter and gave her my advice on what needed changes. I also asked, "Have you thought about why these jobs are not working out". I stated, I'm not blaming you for anything. I just want to understand what is happening.

Leslie had nothing to say which made things even more frustrating. She ended up walking out on the conversation, and I went back to what I was doing.

Meanwhile, the house remained a place of smiles in public, but behind the scenes, I was carrying a weight few saw. The silence was deafening. The laughter was forced.

The distance between us grew, though I held on tightly, afraid to let go of the image we'd built. Friends and church members praised our commitment, unaware of the storm brewing beneath the surface. I was a husband trying to hold everything together, our family, our faith, and the fragile hope that things would get better.

There were small fights that grew, cold silences at night, and a distance in her eyes I couldn't reach. I brushed them aside, telling myself every marriage has struggles. But deep down, I knew we were running on borrowed time. I was strong on the outside because I had to be. For the kids, for the family, and for the community that looked up to us. But inside, the foundation was crumbling.

Now I realize how important it is to listen to those early warnings, the subtle cracks that hint at deeper fractures. Ignoring them only made the fall harder when the truth finally came crashing down. To onlookers, our marriage seemed rock solid. We smiled at church events, posed for family photos, and hosted dinners where laughter filled the rooms.

That night, after the kids were asleep, I found myself sitting alone in the living room listening to the silence grow louder. I sat there with my elbows on my knees, staring at nothing. I thought about the promises we made, the vows to support and love through good times and bad. The thought of my promise to God replayed in my head. I felt lost, struggling to hold on to a marriage slipping through my fingers. My marriage was becoming lonely which was something I never wanted to feel.

As time went on, the pressure showed in other ways than I was expecting. It seemed like the pressure was causing Leslie to need constant reassurance. Whether it was letting her know she would get a job soon or my whereabouts. It was annoying but I did my best not to show it. I wanted people to notice what I was seeing. Leslie withdrew when things didn't go her way. She even started making things feel like a monitoring relationship.

The first time she made me feel monitored was when I went to the gym one day. My phone buzzed and it would be text messages from her. "Are you still at the gym? You've been there for over an hour."

If I told her I was going to watch the game, she would question it like it was suspicious. "You're going by yourself?" she asked once, standing in the doorway like it was a problem. It wasn't the first time I went to the bar to watch the game but she seemed serious about it. "I'm watching the game. I don't need a crowd." However, I do find some other fans and cheer along as the game goes by. That was the easiest way to say it without creating too big of a situation.

There were a few times that she showed up to the places that I was going. I would look up and see her walking in, scanning the room like she was searching for proof of something. Every time, I was exactly where I said I would. Every time, she acted like she had just been checking. I told myself she was just anxious. But in reality, she was being controlling. Her attitude was getting worse as well. It's like she was mad that I was telling the truth and there was nothing to worry about.

I felt understood and seen when others started noticing her attitude.

There was a time when one of my friends pulled me to the side at church, lowering his voice so that no one would hear him. "Bro," he said,

"Your wife doesn't like me." I laughed it off and made him feel like he was tripping. But he was not wrong at all. Leslie had other moments when she would speak to people disrespectfully. I did my best to smooth things over and make excuses as to why she was acting out of the character that they knew. The least I could do was save the embarrassment for the both of us.

In the midst of all of this we were now on our third child and I realize it might be time to have someone help us. So, I said yes when Leslie asked if her parents could move in to help. This happened early in our marriage. Her parents were a great help, especially her mom. She would cook for us every day and wash everyone's clothes. Even cleaned the kitchen, vacuumed, and watched the kids. It was a blessing in the beginning and relieved a lot of pressure off of us. Having her parents around made our days smoother.

Although this was a great addition to our household, I noticed my wife would take advantage of her mom. I would ask why she doesn't help around the house. Her mother is playing the role of a mom and a wife. She was barely working most of the marriage with little part-time jobs here and there.

I started taking care of my own clothes as I felt sorry for her mom. Also, I did not like the drying of some of my nice shirts because they would shrink or I was just getting bigger. I prefer to hang them up. After my wife noticed I was doing my own clothes, she started doing our clothes.

However, it would take her the entire week to do our clothes, and it took her mom half the day. I would tell her the clothes are still everywhere, you want me to finish or when will you finish. She would simply say, "I will finish it." I could sense that she was a little aggravated so I wouldn't rush her too much. Her timing took too long, and I asked her mother to finish it. She knew I liked a clean and nice house.

My wife should have been making sure of that and not depending on her mother to do everything. Her mother spoiled me as well, because I guess I could have cooked too. So, I did. I would BBQ and cook breakfast from time to time.

The longer we lived like that, the more I realized I had become the provider for everybody, my wife, my kids, and her parents. I did not mind providing. I did not mind working. What wore me down was the feeling that no matter how much I carried, it was never enough to create peace.

For most of my marriage, I worked multiple jobs. Not sometimes. All the time. I do not know what it feels like to work just one job and come home and rest. I worked to keep the lights on, to keep the bills paid, to keep the family comfortable, and to keep my wife happy. I worked because I did not want my kids to go without. I worked because I believed that is what a man does. The harder I worked, the more we spent. The more money I earned, the more money disappeared. I kept trying to budget. I kept trying to talk about it. But every conversation turned into tension. At some point, I found myself with six or seven jobs over the years and still feeling like we could not get ahead.

People noticed. "You still working all those jobs?" they asked. I would laugh. "Yeah, I'm staying busy."

Some would joke, "You got a job for each kid." I would smile because I did not want to tell them the truth. I did not want to say I was drowning quietly.

At the same time, our intimacy started to fall apart. I know it was tough because we had a lot of kids and she was tired, which was understandable. Years passed and it got worse, it was barely any sex, and I was like what is going on. She was always tired and exhausted or not really into it. When we would have sex, it was almost as if she would do it just because she knew I wanted it. I had to always initiate the sex as well. I mean, that's what men are supposed to do; however, it is nice when women take advantage of their man as well.

I brought it up to her as this really bothered me. I went to porn to jack off to satisfy myself. A man has his needs, and I'm just saying, especially if his woman is not doing it. One day she caught me jacking off watching porn and she got mad. I questioned her reasoning for getting mad when she wasn't sucking me or making love and having sex.

I end up being addicted to porn cause that's how I got off. Porn only gets you so far, especially when you want the real thing.

I could feel the rejection settling into my body like shame. I tried to talk to Leslie about it again. I tried to be patient. I tried to be understanding. I tried to keep my frustration from turning into bitterness. And I still stayed, because I believed marriage meant you fight. I believed faith meant you endure. I believed leaving was not an option. That is why it still shocks me how blind I was.

I remember one night, Leslie was sitting on the couch scrolling on her phone, smiling at something on the screen. I was across the room watching TV, but something in me noticed the way she angled the phone away. I paused and said casually, "You having fun on your phone texting?" She didn't look up. "It's someone from college." I nodded like it was nothing.

But I remember thinking how differently she would have responded if that were me. If I was texting somebody from college, she would have asked who, how I knew them, and why we were talking. She would have wanted details. But I did not push her because I told myself she would never do anything in front of me, especially text a man in front of me. I told myself she was loyal. I told myself I could trust my wife.

I believed our marriage would only end if cheating happened, and I never believed Leslie was capable of that. She was a homebody. She did not have close friends out here. She rarely went anywhere alone. I used to encourage her to go find friends, to get out, and to enjoy herself with female friends. She always said she did not trust people and preferred to stay close to the family. So, I trusted her. I trusted her so much that when life kept hitting us, I kept saying we could fix it.

When her dreams shifted, I supported each one. When she wanted to start businesses, I funded it. When she wanted to sell products, I paid for supplies. When she wanted school, I helped pay for it. When she wanted to start an agency, I put in over twenty thousand dollars because I believed in her, and because I wanted our family to win.

I will never forget the grand opening. The kids were there. We were smiling. Family and friends were clapping.

Leslie stood in front of everyone shining like she had finally arrived at the life she wanted. When she started thanking people, she thanked her parents first. I stood there clapping slowly, trying to swallow the sting rising in my throat. Then near the end she said, almost like she remembered something she forgot, "Oh, I have to thank my husband."

She completed an entire speech and almost forgot about thanking the one who funded her entire business. Something in me hardened quietly in that moment. I did not cause a scene. I did not say anything. I just smiled because I knew the room was watching, and I had learned how to hold pain behind my teeth.

Less than a year later, federal agents stormed into her agency and arrested her. I did not find out in a dramatic way. I found out through a phone call. My phone rang, and when I answered, it sounded like Leslie was trying to talk through tears. "Terrance," she said, "I'm in jail." I thought it was a joke. I hung up.

Then I called back and it went straight to voicemail. Minutes passed like hours. When she called again, the line clicked and that automated voice came on. The call connected and I heard her breathing. "Leslie," I said, stunned, "What is going on?" Her voice cracked. "They arrested me." All I could ask was the only thing my mind could hold. "What are you doing in jail?"

She started explaining, but my ears were ringing. My whole body felt hot and cold at the same time. I thought about the kids. I thought about her parents in the house. I thought about everything I had done to keep us afloat. I thought about the money, the years, the jobs, and the sacrifices.

I remember sitting there with the phone pressed to my ear, realizing something I was not ready to say out loud yet.

The life I had been fighting to protect was not just under pressure. It was built on something I did not fully understand, and whatever the truth was, it was bigger than what she was telling me on that phone. That was the first time I felt it clearly. Something had been wrong for a long time, and I was about to find out just how deep it went.

CHAPTER 4

MY DAD'S DECLINE

eslie and I had recently celebrated another anniversary when my phone rang. I was working in my shed outside where I work and needed to take a break. I went into the kitchen and open the refrigerator humming to myself and the sound of one of the kids laughing in the next room. The house was loud like it always was, full of movement, and full of life.

I answered the phone and it was my dad. He said Terrance, I am cancer free. I was so excited to hear that. He was diagnosed with cancer earlier that year. He completed treatments and then next thing you know he was cancer free. I was praying for him, and I thanked God he was giving more time to live on this earth.

My dad had been declared cancer-free, and Leslie and I had just celebrated our anniversary like it was a new beginning. Earlier that month on our anniversary she said, "Terrance I know I have not been the best wife, and I want to continue to improve on my behavior, do you still want to spend the rest of your life with me?" I said yes, I would love to spend the rest of my life with you. We kissed and made love. Thank God she cannot have more kids because we would have had another one, or two that night.

I had flown out of state that same month to celebrate with my dad, my siblings, and family members. We sat around a table with him and my siblings, eating, laughing, drinking a little, and playing dominoes like, we always did. My dad was the life of the party, the kind of man who could walk into a room and pull people into joy without trying. Dominoes was his favorite, and he was very good at playing. He made sure we all learned, not by teaching with lectures but by beating us until we got better. Those nights at my dad's house were childhood memories to me. They were home.

My dad had multiple kids while he was married to my mom, but he always wanted us all there as we got older. I live the furthest, so I was the one who was mostly not in the picture physically. I spoke with my dad on the phone to remain in touch and we would go visit 1-2 times a year and bring the kids to spend time with him.

He even flew out my way one year just to spend time with his grandkids and me. When he came of course, we played dominoes and he still beat me up on our best out of seven games. I won three games, so I was happy with that. He just was lucky.

The next month, I was working in my shed and my phone rang. It was my dad; he said I have something I need to share with you all. I was like oh lord what is it, saying to myself. His fiancée was in the background stating it is best he speak with all of us at the same time. I started calling my siblings on three way and adding them to the call.

My siblings weren't all on the line yet, and my dad got impatient and started talking anyway, his voice strong but slightly strained. We cut him off, laughing through it. "Hold on," one of us said. "You wanted all these kids. You need to wait until they get on the phone." My dad chuckled a short laugh that still sounded like him. "Y'all taking too long." We laughed with him.

My dad said his cancer came back and moving very fast and had spread. The laughter left the room very quickly. I was devasted when he said that. I listened with the phone pressed against my ear and my eyes blurred before I could stop it. Tears rolled down my face uncontrollably, and I tried to wipe them away like I could stop what I was hearing. He stated he will be placed in hospice care tomorrow. My heart dropped, I was like this cannot be happening. My dad was only in his early sixties with a whole life ahead of him. Dying was the last thing any of us expected.

When the call ended, I sat there in silence. The house was still making noise around me, but it sounded far away. My chest felt tight like somebody had tied a rope around it and kept pulling. I cried hard, then I prayed hard, because that is what I do when my mind cannot find solid ground. I told myself to be strong and for God to give me strength. That was the first thing I grabbed onto. Terrance, be strong. Not because I felt strong, but because I didn't know what else to be.

After I got myself together, I went into the house and walked into the living room. Leslie looked at me, and knew something was wrong. Some of the kids were nearby, half paying attention, half distracted by life. "What happened?" she asked. I took a deep breath. I swallowed and said it. "My dad's cancer came back." The room shifted. My daughter Lauren looked up immediately, her face serious. Our baby Ilana asked, "Is grandpa okay?" Lauren went quiet and stared at the floor and the tears rolling down her eyes. My wife started crying and then I went to hold them and give them a tissue. By far this broke my heart watching them cry but I knew I had to hold it together.

I went upstairs and shared the news with Jaiden and then I went to Will's room. In a state of jaw dropping shock, they were both trying to control their tears and was sad. I told them it is okay to cry and gave them a hug. Then they both started crying in their rooms.

I went to my youngest son Darien room and told him. I knew he would take it the hardest. So, I had to take a big breath before telling him. He took it very hard, his cries were loud and he just dropped to the floor. I was holding him and just let him cry and let it out. I was about to break down watching him take his death so hard. I still had to remain strong and ask God to help me hold it together for my family.

Darien asked a question so innocent it cut me open. "So… can they fix it like they did the last time?" Ilana didn't understand the words, but she understood the sadness and moved closer to Leslie. I took another breath and said what I did not want to say. "He's not going to make it."

Everyone in the house was sad and crying. Ilana started asking for something, anything, to break the tension. And then the weight fell back on me again, heavy and familiar. Be strong. Be strong for them.

That night, I went in each of the kids' room to check on them and tell them I love them, our nightly routine as usual. When the kids finally went to sleep, I sat on the edge of the bed staring at nothing. Leslie laid beside me scrolling, quiet and texting on her phone. I could feel the distance between us even in the same room. It wasn't a fight. It wasn't loud. It was worse than that. It was quiet and unspoken, like a wall we had both helped build and neither of us knew how to tear down.

I booked the next flight out. Before I left, I prayed again, but this time the prayer was different. It wasn't just about healing. It was about control. God, give me strength. Help me not fall apart. Help me not cry in front of my dad. Help me be what he needs me to be. I thought strength meant silence. I thought strength meant swallowing grief until nobody could see it.

When I arrived, my dad was still my dad. He was thinner and slower, but his humor was still sharp.

He still had that look in his eyes like he could turn any moment into a joke if you gave him the chance. He was sitting up when I walked in, and when he saw me, he smiled. "Well look at you," he said. "You made it." "Yes sir," I replied, forcing myself to control my emotions. "Did you really think I wouldn't show up. That would have been crazy." He nodded like it was obvious. "I'm still here."

I sat down close to him, and for a while we talked like everything was normal. We talked about the kids. We talked about home. We joked a little. The social worker came in, and my dad ask can you give my son some type of form for his job. When he asked her that, I knew he wanted me here. Then the social worker gave me her card.

Then the nurse came in and talked to my dad. When the nurse was leaving, I walked her out. When we were outside I asked the question I was afraid to ask. "How long he has to live?" I said quietly. The hospice nurse didn't hesitate. "Two to three months." It felt like somebody punched the air out of my lungs. My mouth opened, but only two words came out. "My God."

I went back into the room and watched my dad try to live inside a timeline he didn't choose. He started making arrangements so that no one had to think about it. He went plot shopping, picked where he wanted to be buried, and spoke about it with ease, but it broke me in ways I couldn't explain. He said not many people get to plan their funeral. I kept saying be strong, Terrance.

One day a hospice pastor came in, prayed over him, and began to sing softly. The room changed. My dad raised his hands, his voice turning into a whisper prayer.

I watched him and felt something I didn't expect. Peace. It wasn't the peace of everything will be okay. It was the peace of its time. For a moment, my faith held me up like a beam. To live is Christ. To die is gain. I repeated it inside my head like a scripture shield.

Then my dad looked at me and smirked. "Alright. I don't like company." I laughed because I knew what he meant. He wanted rest. He wanted space. He wanted control over his last days. Even dying, he wanted things his way. I flew out there again and again, sometimes twice a month. I helped with medication. I sat with him. I tried to manage the tension between what he wanted and what he needed. Sometimes he'd ask for more meds, and I'd tell him not yet. He would frown. "Son, you trying to be my boss?" His fiancée laughed later and told me what he said after I left the room. "He came out here and tried to be the boss of me." We laughed, and she said he likes that, but inside, I was breaking.

While I was traveling back and forth, life kept moving forward. The kids still needed rides. Meals still needed to happen. Bills still needed to be paid. Leslie still had her moods. Our marriage still had its gaps. The grief didn't replace our problems. It piled on top of them. I still told myself I was being strong, but I was also getting numb, which has a cost.

I flew my whole family out to see my dad while he was still moving around. The kids sat close to him, awkward at first, then more comfortable. I watched my dad smile at them and saw a flicker of the life return to his face. He played with Ilana and she was laughing and smiling. All I was thinking, at the moment, was that my little baby girl will never remember her grandfather.

I was crushed again but holding it down by being strong for everyone else. We flew back home at the end of the week as the kids had to get back to school.

A week later, my phone rang again. "Come now," my uncle said. "He won't make it through the weekend." I remember standing still, staring at the wall, trying to move and not being able to. I started searching flights like a man trying to outrun death. But getting there wasn't simple. It took multiple connections, then a long drive to my hometown.

I called my dad while I was trying to figure it out. "Daddy," I said. "I'm coming. I'll be there tomorrow morning." He didn't answer. My dad always answered me. The silence told me what the words didn't.

That night, I prayed, not a long prayer, not an eloquent one, just the kind of prayer that comes from the bottom of the heart. God, please. Less than thirty minutes later, the phone rang again. "Daddy died." I sat there holding the phone, and not a single tear fell from my eyes. I thought the tears would come like a wave and knock me down, but nothing came. I felt hollow. I felt like my grief had been locked behind a door inside me, and I didn't know how to open it. I told myself he was at peace and the pain was gone. I told myself the storm was over. To live is Christ. To die is gain. I repeated it again.

We all come into this world living to eventually die. We all have an expiration date; some of us know when it comes and some of us do not. After losing one of my twins, she was almost six weeks old. I knew then that we are not meant to live forever in this world. To live is Christ and to die is gain. My daddy went on to see my oldest daughter Nevaeh.

The next day, I flew in and drove for hours to get to where they had his body. When I walked into the funeral home, the air felt cold and heavy. I stood there and looked at him lying still, peaceful like he was taking a nap. It didn't look real. I leaned in and whispered, "Rest in peace, Daddy." Still no tears. I held my grief like a man holding a burning coal in his bare hand and pretending it wasn't burning.

My dad had always been proud of me. He would always tell me that I was a great father. When I earned my doctorate degree, he laughed and said, "I guess that means I'm a doctor too since we have the same name." I honored him the only way I knew how. I spoke at his funeral with no tears, and I gave him an honorary doctorate in front of the people who loved him. I praised God through the pain. I stood tall. I stayed composed. I performed strength, but inside, something in me was starting to crack.

During that same season, while I was flying back and forth and trying to keep my family together, Leslie told me she was going to Homecoming with her friend. The timing struck a nerve in me. It didn't feel like the right moment for anything extra. My life felt like it was unraveling. I looked at her and tried to understand. "Homecoming?" I repeated. "I never go anywhere," she said. "I just want to hang out with my best friend." Part of me wanted to say now, really, but I was too overwhelmed to argue. I had encouraged her years ago to find friends and go out, so I swallowed my discomfort and said okay go and have fun. It was easier to swallow things than to confront them. That was my pattern.

When we gathered with family at my grandmother's house after my dad passed, another crack appeared, one that didn't belong to grief alone. My sister walked into the house with her male friend, and the energy shifted in a way everyone could feel. My two brothers' wives did not speak to her. They didn't say hello. They didn't offer condolences. They didn't even acknowledge her presence. One walked right past her like she didn't exist. Another got up and went outside like she couldn't stand to be in the room.

My sister sat down quietly, trying to hold her dignity, trying not to fall apart in front of people who were already treating her like she didn't deserve basic respect. I watched it happen, and something in my chest tightened. I was hurt for my sister, but I was also hurt at the reality of how family can fail you when you need them most. Right after we left my grandmother, my sister brought it up and cried. We all noticed how her sister in laws treated her, it was very obvious. I couldn't imagine Leslie ever ignoring my sister like that in a moment like this, but I also knew my marriage wasn't built on the kind of support I kept pretending we had.

While I was out there working on funeral arrangements, I asked Leslie to sing at my dad's funeral. I asked her to sing, "To Live is Christ and to Die is Gain." I just could not get those words out of my mind. She prepared the song while I was out of state with the family. On Friday night, Leslie and the kids flew in. On Saturday, she sang, and it was beautiful. I stood up and praised God when she finished, because for a moment, her voice made the room feel cared for.

After the funeral and repast, we went to my uncle's house to be with family that night, but Leslie stayed behind at my mom's house. She didn't grieve with us. She didn't hold space the way I expected a wife to hold it. Later, she came to pick up the kids, and when she arrived, her face looked different. The look in her eyes wasn't sadness. It was something sharper. Fire in her eyes.

She didn't even try to check on how my family was doing. It was like she had stepped into the moment wearing anger instead of empathy. I stared at her, confused. "You're not going to get out?" I asked. She made an excuse and she stayed in the car like she didn't want to be near anyone.

That was when I started to realize something dangerous about the way I had been living. Strength wasn't saving me. It was silencing me, and the silent parts of me were starting to rot. I didn't know it then, but the man I became during my father's death would be the same man who would soon be forced to face betrayal, not just as pain, but as proof, proof that the life I was holding together was already falling apart while I was busy trying not to cry. And the worst part was this. I still believed I had no idea what was coming next.

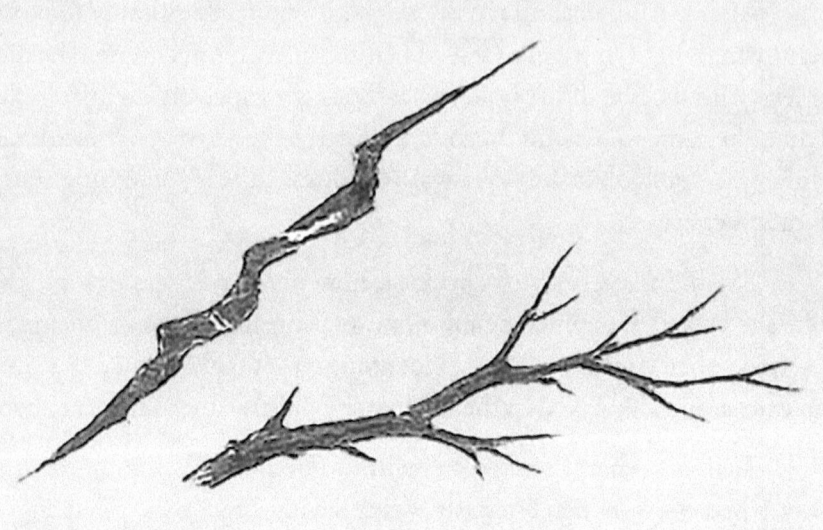

PART II

THE BETRAYALS

CHAPTER 5

THE SPIRIT OF DISCERNMENT (SOMETHING IS OFF)

When I came home after burying my father, the house felt familiar but strangely foreign, like I had stepped back into a life that had continued without me. Grief has a way of sharpening your senses, making you notice things you might have once overlooked. The first thing I noticed was Leslie constantly on her phone. It was always in her hand, at the kitchen counter, in the hallway, and in the car long after she pulled into the driveway.

One night I walked outside after hearing her pull into the driveway. The car was already off, and her face was being lit by the light of her phone screen.

She clearly intended to finish her conversation before coming into the house. I tapped lightly on the window, and she jumped, not startled but jolted. "Hey sweetie. You, ok?" I asked. She responded with a suspicious quickness. "Yes, just taking care of some bills." I didn't question it and went back into the house. My chest tightened as I got closer to the house. Bills don't make people jump like that.

Weeks later before my father's funeral I walked by the front door and saw that she was still in the car. It was around four in the evening which didn't make sense. She worked half days at this point so four o'clock was strange. When I went to check on her to see if everything was alright. She said, "Yes, that was Alisha and we were talking about homecoming, so I wanted to finish my thoughts before getting out. Is that a problem" The attitude didn't shock me, but she also could have picked up a couple of the other kids from school.

In the weeks after my father's death, life did not slow down to accommodate my grief. Jaiden needed rides, Will had school commitments, Lauren had events, Darien needed help with homework, and little Ilana still wanted bedtime stories and for her daddy to take her a bath. So, I moved through each day on exhaustion and prayer, handling school drop-offs, pickups, practices, groceries, and work. Leslie, meanwhile, seemed increasingly elsewhere, physically present but emotionally unreachable.

One afternoon I asked if she was coming to Lauren's school event. She didn't look up from her phone. "You can go," she said. I studied her for a moment. "Everything alright?" "Yeah," she replied. "Just talking to Alisha about homecoming."

My father had just died, and my world still felt cracked open, yet her energy was fixed on a trip. "I thought maybe we could go to the Super 10 game in Texas this year," I said carefully. "It's around my birthday that is coming up. Might be good for us... get away together." She shrugged slightly. "You can go by yourself." The phrase echoed longer than it should have. "I wanted to go with you," I said quietly. Flights were expensive anyway, so I let it drop, but something inside me whispered to pay attention.

I just found it strange that all her time and energy was to her phone and not the family. I was doing everything, running around with the kids like crazy right after I buried my dad. She did not even grieve with me, pray with me, or ask me how I was feeling. She did not ask what she could do to help or even just give me a hug and some sympathy. Leslie never showed any signs of caring about what I was going through.

I was always there for her throughout all her medical treatments, always motivating her, and trying to help her with her self-esteem. Every time I would walk into the room where she was, she would jump. To myself, I was like what is she jumping for. I've been on my weight loss journey, so I know I did not get fat, and my face never changed to look scary to her. She brought up going to homecoming and how she was so excited to hang out with her friend.

She said this was her first girls' trip since we got married. I told her it felt strange that she wanted to go to homecoming so bad at the time of my dad's death. She said her friend asked and couldn't say no. I responded, "Okay, well, I hope you all have so much fun."

The next morning confirmed everything. I woke up earlier than usual, it was still dark out. To me Leslie was still in the bed so I didn't even check to see if she was there or not. The main bathroom door was closed, and then I noticed the toilet area door was closed, something we never did in our house. I opened it, and Leslie screamed, "I'm using the bathroom! What do you want?"

She dropped her right hand down fast when I opened the door. She had an item in that hand as well. Her phone was sitting sideways on the laundry basket, the screen glowing. I saw she was live with someone on the phone. I said nothing and stepped back, using the kids' bathroom instead. A few minutes later she appeared in the hallway, her voice suddenly gentle. "You need to go? I'm done." "I already did," I replied, but my spirit was unsettled.

I walked out to my home office, closed the door behind me, and prayed. I said, "God, my wife is up to something. Please reveal to me what she is doing." I knew she wasn't cheating because she's a virtuous, faithful Christian who prays daily and attends church every Sunday. However, something was off with her, and I needed to know.

Let me backtrack before the next session. I always felt that someone was against me for years, but I just did not know who, what, or why. I always prayed that God would please remove any negative energy, people, or individuals from my life who are not for me. Move any spirits of jealousy, envy, and people who are trying to hurt me. I asked God to also bless me with the spirit of discernment and to show me who is meant to be in my life.

Within thirty minutes of praying to God to reveal to me what my wife is doing. It was revealed to me. I was like this cannot be real. My wife and I share our email accounts so we can help each other with our businesses. She has access to my stuff. All the accounts where I pay the bills, she has access to, and I do not have access to it. However, when you trust your spouse, there's no need to look at everything, right?

When I logged into one of my Gmail accounts for work, it redirected to her account, and I saw the messages she was sending to a man. My hand froze on the mouse. There were songs, love notes, images, words of their love and how strong it was. She was sending him daily messages, singing with all her heart. My breathing shortened as I scrolled.

Each message felt like glass sliding into my chest. She had sent one while I was sitting beside my dying father, another the day I flew home, another the morning after. My hands began shaking so violently I had to grip the desk. "Lord…" I whispered. I could not believe this was real;

this was to me a joke, there is no way my wife is cheating on me. Maybe it was emotional, maybe it was harmless, maybe I was misunderstanding.

She was sharing how her love for him was so strong, even though he lives in Houston, Texas. I could not believe my eyes and what I was hearing. My wife is really in love with another man. Then I saw his name.

My fraternity brother James. A married man and a man I had vouched for to make the fraternity line. Something inside me broke silently. I didn't shout, didn't throw anything, didn't collapse. I prayed.

"Thank you, God, for revealing this," I said, though the words tasted bitter. But the revelation wasn't finished. A quiet thought pressed into my mind telling me to go upstairs. I went.

At the side of the bed was the item I had seen in her right hand that day in the restroom. The item was a pink vibrator. My wife was on live video naked with a married man and using a vibrator to please herself while he watched. The evidence erased the final refuge of denial. My knees weakened, and I sat down slowly. My marriage, the life I believed I was protecting, had been collapsing while I was planning a funeral, while I was praying, while I was trying to stay strong for everyone.

Later that day, I was working in my office with one of my several jobs. I received a text message from our cell phone provider stating to login to the account. I went upstairs to get the information needed from Leslie, and she was texting on the phone. I asked for the login to the phone provider account because of the message I received. She informed me that it was our son Jaiden who was trying to get something, but she fixed it. I said okay, but I still want to log in to make sure everything is alright.

She said, "Why are you stressing over that? I told you I fixed it. Don't let that worry you so badly. "I just want to check," I said calmly. She did not want to give me access to our account, although I pay all the bills. She was making excuses. She then said I forgot the password. I went to the website and clicked forgot password. I asked her what she would like to change the password to. She gave me a smart-mouth response and said, what I usually have.

I pretended not to know what that could be. But she insisted I had nothing to stress over or worry about. I questioned why there is such a big deal about you not wanting to give me the password to our account. I had already seen the email, so I already knew what was going on behind my back.

However, I was still in awe and couldn't believe it was true. Maybe I am overreacting because she is cheating on me with my fraternity brother. I looked into the account from my phone while she was texting on her phone. I knew she was texting him. I continued to act calm, briefly looked at the call log, then logged off.

She said, "You see, it's nothing. I told you I fixed it." Our son was trying to order something. I said okay, good night love, and she said, goodnight love you too. I went to bed, and she stayed on her phone.

The next day, I went to log into our account and noticed she had changed the password. I could not log in. I texted her at work for the new password. She said I did not change it. I said that I could not log in.

I clicked the forgot password button again. The code went to her phone, and she gave it to me to create another password. I put the same password she uses. That day, I saw all the call logs for three numbers she had been talking to for a very long time. One was a very long period, and all day for weeks.

I entered all three numbers in a search online and the familiar names I knew came up. She was constantly on the phone with her best friend who lives in Texas, her cousin, and future husband for long periods of time daily.

When I look at the text time log, she was texting nonstop during instructional hours while teaching students. My fraternity brother was sending her naked pictures of himself during instructional hours while students were present in her classroom. I brought him into the fraternity and voted for him. I could not believe it, as he was my fraternity brother and Facebook friend, and we belonged to the same fraternity group page.

Brotherhood, I thought bitterly. So much for that. My chest tightened until breathing felt like work, yet I stayed quiet, still gathering, still processing, and still hoping I was somehow wrong.

I saw the emails and all the text messages. I was in awe, my heart beating fast and could not believe what I was reading. I saw this on her phone by just looking in the drawer. Finding this phone was the game charger. It was also the cherry on top of everything.

Even though I thought I had seen it all, there was a time when she proved me wrong. Maybe I had to understand that Leslie was not always using the bathroom for what I thought. To her it was the perfect place to hide from me. She was on the toilet and had the door shut.

What devastated me most wasn't just the affair. It was the timing. While my father was dying, while I was burying him, while I was trying not to collapse in front of my children, she was building another life. Texting him at my dad's funeral all day. I was shaking like a leaf. The day I found out felt like the ground shifted beneath me, pulling me into a chasm I never thought I'd face.

The betrayal didn't feel loud; it felt surgical, precise, like my reality had been cut open without anesthesia. Sleep abandoned me, and nights became replay loops of conversations, memories, and small moments now poisoned with new meaning. How long? How deep? How did I miss this? But an even heavier question followed me into the dark, who am I if the life I built isn't real?

At first, denial tried to protect me. I told myself it couldn't be true, that the signs were misleading. But the evidence was undeniable. The emails, the secret meetings, the whispered conversations when I wasn't around. Everything confirmed the nightmare I was trying to block out.

The emotional toll was crushing. I felt every betrayal in my bones, anger, confusion, grief, and a deep, aching sadness. It wasn't just about infidelity; it was about broken promises, shattered trust, and the loss of the family I thought we had. I wrestled with questions that had no answers.

How could someone I loved so deeply hurt me this way? How could a man I called my fraternity brother betray that bond? The betrayal wasn't just personal; it felt like an assault on my identity, my values, and my entire world. The nights were the hardest. Alone with my thoughts, I replayed memories, searching for signs I missed, moments I wish I could change.

Sleep became elusive, replaced by waves of pain and disbelief. My wife brought shame and humiliation. I felt trapped in silence, isolated by the betrayal. Despite the darkness, a small part of me clung to hope; the hope that there was a way forward, that healing was possible even after such profound hurt. But in those early days, hope felt fragile, almost impossible to grasp.

The affair was not just a secret kept behind closed doors; it was a wound that would redefine my life, challenge every belief, and force me to confront pain I never imagined.

One evening after work, I sat on the edge of the bed speaking about something that had always mattered to me. "I want our kids to inherit more than struggle," I told her. "I've been working toward generational wealth... something lasting." I said to her, I have been working on trying to make sure our kids have something left from us when they get older and when we die. I have been expressing to her for years about generational wealth and how we can achieve it.

I want the best for all our kids. Right after I said all of this sincerely. She listened quietly, then said something that split the air. She told me she doesn't think we should be married anymore, and that she had a wonderful time with me, and that she wanted me to be happy. Her words were calm, practiced, as if rehearsed. She basically ignored everything I said and had the attitude of, "Well, guess what, you do not have to worry about my budget or generational income, I am out because I have a new husband coming soon." All the while, she did not know I was on to her.

She did not know I had already seen the email and the messages I found. I listened to her, engaged with her, and questioned her to see if she was going to talk about her future husband, another woman's current husband. She did not mention that it was another person or him at all. She was mainly saying that I haven't been happy for a long time, and she wants to make me happy.

Meanwhile, I was not unhappy with her as I was dealing with the loss of my dad, and she had just asked me if I wanted to spend the rest of my life with her during our anniversary trip.

When she came clean about her spending, it felt like she really didn't care. Her response was, "I messed up with the money over the years; I admit it." It seemed like she was brushing it off.

Leslie said she felt she shouldn't be here and wanted to take herself out of the world after my letter of trying to work things out last year. She talked to the pastor about what happened. Said she was not the best person and wanted to be better. She didn't know that these words would stick with her the way they did. It was like my mind kept a recording of it, she stated. I couldn't believe what she was saying, but I was interested in hearing more.

Leslie stated, I do not feel like I am a bad person, I do care and try my best to do things the right way. My strategies are often not the right way. I cannot argue about that. For the sake of sanity, your happiness, and you not stressing, I do not know if I need to continue with you stressing from me. Last year's letter really bothered me. I tried and wanted to make it work.

I do not yell at you or raise my voice much, and I got better with communication. I have a way of getting loud with people, that's how I am, but it's not intentional. I do not know if it will continue working. I do not feel like I will do the right things, honestly. I do not see it changing for you. You'll continue to see the past and things I mess up on.

I like to eat; if I were a man, I would at least feel like my wife is not going hungry. Okay, it was a joke, I was trying to lighten the mood. I could not get the words from your letter out of my head. I felt like maybe we were not meant to be married; we were not meant to be in a relationship. I loved you as a friend, and we had fun together.

I said we have been married for 18 years, why would you stay all these years? Leslie stated, I mean, we were not meant to stay married after going through the same thing repeatedly. She was saying this with so much pride and confidence. Her face looked like she had hit the jackpot. Leslie stated, after the last few years, you said you weren't happy. The way you put it last year, you never put it that way before. It made me feel like the bad times were just me. You had no part in anything, and that I caused the bad times.

It's not the fact that I want to divorce you, I feel like if I remove myself from the puzzle, you will be stress-free and happy. I see you; I hear you, and I know that you are not happy. I see you trying.

As she continued to talk, there was so much frustration building up inside of me. It gave me all the confidence I needed to speak up about how I was feeling. Except this time, I didn't hold back any of my emotions.

I stated you scream and yell at me in front of your parents and the kids. Your dad curses in front of the kids. Your dad is so rude at the dinner table, but you say nothing about it. We can't watch TV because it's your mom's TV at this point. The crazy part is that your parents get a lot of respect and appreciation, as if they aren't always disrespecting me.

Your mom literally cooks for him and only him many times, yet I pay all the bills and take care of them. I told your mom to tell him to stop cursing in front of the kids. She told him what I said, and he said I need to mind my business. How wild does that sound to you because you never do anything when I say something.

You're not in love anymore, and you want a divorce, so nothing I can do about it. You were already feeling some type of way about this since you are bringing it up while I am talking about creating a budget and watching our spending. You would think you want things for yourself and generational wealth for your kids. All I said was to help fix us, and you are giving up.

She said you give me nice things and I am appreciated. I said, but now you want to divorce me. Because you want me to be happy, I am confused about that. That's weird, last year you wrote me notes regarding us, and then I wrote the letter, so why didn't you leave me then? The room grew quiet after I asked that question. She didn't say anything about her affair, although I knew.

I studied her face, searching for remorse, hesitation, anything. There was none. When I asked, "Have you ever cheated on me?" She answered smoothly, "No, I love you". The lie didn't shock me; what shocked me was how easily it came. When she said she loved me, I realized something chilling, love and truth are not always companions.

I stated for the past 18 years, I never cheated or wanted to cheat and she stated me neither. I stated most men who are making all the money, paying all the bills, taking care of someone else's parents, would have been cheated on you when he is not getting sex from his wife.

Last year, you said you wanted to make it work, then for our anniversary, three months ago, you asked me if I wanted to spend the rest of my life with you and now you are telling me you are not in love with me anymore.

Leslie stated, I am in love with you. But I knew she was in love with someone else. She had so much confidence in her voice as she was speaking to me. If she only knew that her life was about to change drastically.

Leslie stated, your mom said she would have some Louis Vuitton bags and all kinds of stuff if you were her husband. Your mom and I laughed and had a good time about that. I told her that doesn't mean anything to me. I stated, yet you put all these expensive things on your list for me to buy. You do not appreciate the things I do for you nor show it.

That night I lay awake beside the woman I once believed was heaven-sent and realized something with terrifying clarity. The betrayal didn't begin when I discovered it. It began long before, in the small silences, the dismissed concerns, the emotional distance we both learned to live inside. As I stared into the darkness, one truth settled heavily into my chest. The life I was fighting to hold together was already gone. I just hadn't stopped long enough to see it. But now I had, and there was no going back.

CHAPTER 6

THE AFFAIR

I was sleeping with the enemy, and the realization settled over me like a quiet storm I could not outrun. After I read all of the messages, I immediately wanted to confront Leslie, demand the truth. But something inside me said it was not the time. I prayed and prayed like I have never prayed before.

I prayed harder than I had ever prayed before, asking God for wisdom, restraint, and clarity. It is a special kind of torment to sleep with someone who is betraying you while they continue to act as if nothing has changed. She still told me she loved me, still moved through the house with familiar ease, yet I knew those same words were being given to a married man.

A couple days after, I had to attend an out-of-state conference for work. She told me to text her when my plane lands. I said I would, just like I always had. I called and then FaceTime her to show her my nice room, like I usually do when I traveled. She loves to see the hotel rooms. She smiled, asked about the flight, and told me to enjoy the conference. I was so glad I was attending the conference because I needed that time away to get myself together. I sat on the edge of the bed and broke.

The tears came fast and without warning. I cried my heart out in my room. I cried for the years I believed we were building something sacred. I cried for the promises we made. I felt like I wasted almost twenty years of my life with the woman who promised till death do us part and who asked me three months ago, will I continue to spend the rest of my life with her.

After crying so much, I check my work emails to get my mind off this for a little while. I went to take a shower and refresh. When I got in the shower, I just broke down and got on my knees crying uncontrollably. After the tears came prayer. "God, give me the strength to move forward," I whispered into the emptiness.

When the crying and praying stopped, a strange calm followed. It was not peace. It was resolve.

I began to investigate quietly, carefully, documenting what I had seen. I planned my emails and letters. I took notes, planning my next steps. I even looked for all the people who might have witnessed or been involved.

It was very difficult to enjoy the conference because my mind was focusing on the plan. But I forced myself to remain present when I could. Occasionally, learning and conversation distracted me long enough to breathe. Each night I still called the kids, told them I loved them, and asked about their day. Fatherhood did not pause for heartbreak.

Before flying back home, I had everything planned out, though I still did not know when or how it would unfold. The only thing to do was wait for the perfect time. When I arrived home, we celebrated Jaiden's birthday at a venue filled with laughter and music. He ran around with his friends, carefree, exactly as a child should be. I watched him and reminded myself to stay composed. Leslie smiled widely, appearing light and joyful. Yet even in the middle of the celebration, her phone remained close, her attention drifting toward it again and again. I kept my composure, speaking when spoken to, laughing when appropriate, and carrying the secret alone.

In the days that followed, her excitement about homecoming intensified. She kept saying, "This is my first girls' trip and I am excited." It's like she could have cared less that my dad just died. She never asked me if I was okay, needed therapy, needed someone to talk to, nothing. She never prayed with me and never offered the comfort of a simple embrace.

She was just so happy about going to homecoming. However, I knew exactly what she was really happy to do.

She was always posting pictures of herself on her Instagram stories, showing how happy she was. She was having the time of her life cheating on me. I just watched it all. I even liked her pictures and commented on her stories.

One evening, while she was out, I noticed items laid carefully in her suitcase when I was going to take a shower. Among the clothes were gifts she had prepared. One of them she handmade for him. My chest tightened, though I didn't physically react. When I asked about her travel details, the answers shifted.

I did not see her purchase the flight, hotel room, or anything else. So, I asked her how she got the flight and the hotel room. Where are you all staying? She told me that Alisha paid for it and she Zelle her some money as well. I asked who was picking her up from the Texas airport.

One moment a friend had arranged things, then her cousin, Kierra was the final person to pick her up. The inconsistencies stacked quietly in my mind. I realized I did not know where she was staying, who was picking her up, or even the basic structure of the trip. Still, I held my questions close.

I went upstairs and opened her drawer by the bed. I saw the phone and put it in my back pocket. When she left home heading to the airport, I revisited the evidence, moving carefully so nothing would alert her. What I saw confirmed what my spirit had already begun to accept, the communication had simply moved elsewhere, hidden behind new channels and private exchanges. I sat there for a long time, staring at the screen, letting the reality settle fully into my bones.

I saw when he was sending her messages, and when she responded. One of the messages I know he sent was a naked picture because he said, I have something sexy to show you of me. I had to get off the app because it was going to vanish, and they would have known something was off. She responded with emojis.

I had to be careful. I saw when he was arriving, which terminal he was waiting at, and him saying, "I cannot wait to see you, baby," and all kinds of sexual things they were going to do.

She texted me when she landed and when she was heading out. I said Kierra is there to pick you up and she confirmed. I asked her to tell Kierra I said hello.

Of course, she said that her cousin said hello. I already saw he was picking her up. Yet information told a different story. Watching the contradictions unfold was surreal, like standing outside my own life and observing it from a distance. My wife forgot to turn off her location, so I could see everywhere she was going. She meets him at his hotel. This was not the hotel where her cousin was staying. I called her as she was leaving as our little girl Ilana was still sick.

Our daughter wanted to Facetime her, but my wife didn't want to answer the phone or respond. I called the hotel where her future husband was staying. I asked them to transfer me to James Harris's room. They asked for the room number, and I said I did not know.

I explained that it is an emergency. The representative transferred me to the room, but of course, he did not answer. However, it confirmed he was staying at the hotel.

I called the hotel again and asked if they could go knock on his door, as I needed to reach him. I told them I was his brother.

I mean, I am his fraternity brother. They would not go. She finally Facetimed my daughter and me outside his hotel. I asked my wife what they had been doing, and she said they went to have a drink. Then she said, I don't feel good. I started asking more questions, and she gave me more excuses for why Kierra wasn't there. She just kept lying and lying, and it was funny to hear them.

She tried to get me off the phone while she was on the way back to the hotel, but I insisted on continuing to stay on the line till her cousin got there. Apparently, her cousin was meeting her at the hotel so they could go somewhere together. She made up some excuse and hung up before the car arrived.

When she arrived at the hotel, I texted her asking to FaceTime me. She would not, she said, because the people in the room are sleeping. Then someone was taking a shower in the bathroom, which had nothing to do with her being on the phone. I asked to speak with her cousin. She said her cousin didn't want to speak to me.

She was upset that I wasn't letting her enjoy her girls' trip. I was just calling because our sick daughter wanted to Facetime her mom. She expressed that her cousin was becoming upset that I wouldn't get off the phone, but that didn't add up since she was also a mom. She would not let me talk to her.

She eventually FaceTime with just her face close to the phone. I said let me tell your cousin hello and let me see her.

She would not and said she does not want to talk. The lies just kept coming, and many of them didn't make sense.

A couple of months before, she had flown out to Lake Mason in Texas with Darien and Ilana and her mom to go visit a family member around the time of my dad being sick. We just went out of state, and she has never flown anywhere without me. I knew something was up in my spirit when she said she was going to go to Texas for a gathering. We've been living out of state for almost 20 years, she has never just wanted to go out of state for a gathering. She didn't even fly out and bring her dad to his brother's funeral.

As the conversation continued between my wife and a frat brother, they sent links to songs and expressed their desire to see each other again. He told her that he wanted to see her again and she responded soon. The next day, she flew out to her so-called gathering with the family, but I knew she was really going to see him.

He also sent her hundreds of dollars. I am assuming that was to fly her to Texas to sleep with him. I never saw a trace of her trip in my accounts. Although she constantly sent herself money from my account to her CashApp/Zelle or her personal account.

There were also messages from the day before my dad's funeral. These messages hurt the most. I wished that I had never seen them. That she really wasn't this type of person. She was really practicing her song in front of him like it was for his dad. Showing him something that was supposed to be for me, for my dad. I never knew people could be like this.

She sends him the video of her singing her heart out at my dad's funeral later that day. I was crushed. She never sent me the video. She said, it must not have gone through. She'll send it again in a minute. To this day, I have yet to receive the video. I can honestly say the song was very touching and I stood up in church in front of hundreds and praised God.

I could not believe she shared a picture of him with her mom. Her mom stated she remembers you very well and she see that you care. She was planning her next steps, and she did not want her mother to be surprised when she marries another man.

One weekend they were talking and my frat brother was out for the night. These were the drunk texts. He would text her a lot when he was out drunk. It was actually interesting knowing how different she was with him. She never liked when I used to drink a lot.

We share notes with each other on the phone, I saw the notes regarding her plan to remarry, be a big family together, putting her parents in assisted living, and how she was going to wait until I fly out of the country for a work trip the next year to leave me. She prayed to God that when the time is right, to grant her all the strength and wisdom she needs. She prayed to God that there is no drama and for a smooth transition between both parties in the might name of Jesus when the time is right.

The plotting, the scheming, the betrayal hit me so hard. How could anyone have an affair with a married person and at the same time while their spouse dad is dying and died. How could the one I gave my heart to break my heart so bad?

The emotional toll was immense. Anger rose and fell in waves, followed by grief, confusion, and a deep sadness that seemed to settle behind my ribs. I replayed memories, searching for signs I might have missed. Sleep became difficult, replaced by long stretches of thought in the dark. I wrestled with questions that had no immediate answers. I would find myself reading the text message between Leslie and James trying to figure out why they would do this to my kids and me.

How could the woman I loved step so far outside the vows we shared? How could a bond I once trusted feel suddenly unfamiliar? This was something I would have never imagined my wife would do. A virtuous woman is a crown to her husband: But she that maketh ashamed is as rottenness in his bones. (Proverbs 12:4 KJV). She is rotten in my bones. I have lost all respect for her for what she did to me, our five kids, and her parents. The way I felt during that time was as if she were dead to me.

She did not even exist in my mind. I never wanted to see her again. We have five kids together, so obviously I have to see her and have some kind of communication when it is dealing with the kids only. This is still very hard for me, as I do not even want to look at her because she has rottenness in my bones. My wife even reached out to my mom; she volunteered information.

She claimed things weren't going well with us. My mom questioned why we weren't doing so great. My wife told her that she would tell her later and not to mention it to me. She offered to call her when she got home and told my mom that she loved her. My mother said that she wouldn't tell me nothing and I love you so much.

My mom told her to ask God to silence every word that was spoken over you that did not come from Him. Pray that anything rooted in darkness be canceled in the name of Jesus, removed from your spirit, and erased from your memory today and forever. Trust that He has the power to do it. Amen.

I prayed this very prayer when I chose to welcome his father back into my life, believing things could be different. Sadly, he never changed, but God still gave me the strength, clarity, and wisdom to move forward.

When I saw my mother text this to her, I was so upset. My mother never told me. Could you imagine if my wife's scheme had made it to the end, how everyone would have left me out?! My mother never told me anything, not a word, not if everything was alright with anyone, I mean nothing. I could never do this to any of my kids, putting their spouse before my blood.

My mother immediately thought it was me cheating and never bothered to check with me, and said do not tell your wife, but I wanted to check in with you. After finding all the messages, I told my mom not to tell my wife anything about what I am about to say. She said I promise I won't. I asked her if my wife reached out to her about anything, and she replied no why? I told her, I am your son, you need to trust your son, do not tell her you are speaking to me about something, what did she tell you?

My mother was acting lost and never said a word after I kept asking her. While I was on the phone with her, she was texting my wife that I was texting her about something. At that point, I was upset and lost all trust from my own mother.

I told her not to reach out to her and she did. When it was time for my soon to be ex to tell more of whatever lie she was going to tell my mother, she did not tell her.

I did not tell my mom what was all going on that day because I could not trust her not to tell my wife. I eventually shared with my mom the evidence of my wife's affairs and that I needed her. She flew out for a few days to be with me. I do appreciate that! I showed her everything. My mom said, wow, you are a good man, your dad would have strangled her. Oh, I know most men would have done a lot of damage to her if they were me, especially all the sacrifices I made for her.

Since we were Facebook friends, I just went to his page and found his wife's page, which gave me all the information that I needed. I found out where my frat brother, his wife, and her cousin's husband work. I sent them all informational emails. I called her best friend's husband as well to see if I could find anything out. He stated he blocked my wife a long time ago after he saw her and his wife talking badly about him. I called the wife's job, no answer. I called another number and they gave me her cell phone number.

I told his wife and sent her text messages. We spoke, and I shared with her that they are driving to the hotel. She asked should I drive there now with a shaking voice. I said no. You will miss them. You need to go wait in the hotel parking lot.

She went to the hotel to catch them. She brought her family members as well. His wife confronted her husband. They didn't even get out of the car, and she began to question him. He told his wife he was dropping a friend back from the airport. Little did he know that his wife knew everything. The lies continued.

His wife told me her husband said she was going to commit suicide, and he was talking to her. Again, Leslie gave more lies and shame to use suicide for someone to feel sorry for her after getting caught having an affair with a married man.

I told his wife that this took me by surprise because she wanted to fuck your husband last night, and suddenly, she wants to kill herself. She is lying. I told her to look at what both said in the text messages sexually. That does not sound like someone who wanted to commit suicide suddenly. His wife shared pictures of them with me after they were caught at the hotel. The hotel workers were in shock looking at the scene. At this point, I was furious.

In fact, there was nothing else more I needed to see or hear. I cut off the ring doorbell, changed the locks, and put her parents in a hotel until she finds them an assisted living place. This is where she was putting them, per her messages.

She told our son she picked up her parents from that hotel because it was in a trashy area. I packed her clothes and put all her stuff out of the house, since she no longer wanted to be married or stay there. She said she was marrying him in writing and sent it to him, so she could now go meet him not when I fly out the country the next year for work.

I then blocked my frat brother on Facebook after his wife caught him with my wife at the hotel. I had already written him a letter to inform him of what he did.

Do you think he apologized? No, he did not, and he never responded to the email. I know for a fact he received it as well.

He then tries to file a domestic restraining order against me as if we were in a relationship and I was violent towards him. The judge dismissed his false charges. He was just embarrassed. I emailed him at his job and copied his managers. He should be charged for lying with the court system.

Also, he should be hit with a homewrecker charge and a charge of alienation of affection. He should also be removed from the fraternity. As a matter of fact, he should just apologize for what he did, so evil won't continue to hunt him.

I also prepared a letter and shared it with her cousin, who considers herself a Christian, woman of God. Her cousin was involved and knew what was going on. I also pulled the phone records and noticed how long she was on the phone with her cousin.

Once everything was said and done with everyone else, I emailed her. It was obvious that she had received the letter, because when I came home, there was a huge scene. I left the house because my wife's mother forgot her medicine bag. As I was almost out of the neighborhood, her mother called back, saying she had found the bag she was looking for. I felt like they played me again. When I went back to the house, the cops were already there, and she was trying to leave with the kids.

I asked her why are you trying to take the kids away from me. I was upset about this. Then my youngest daughter was sad, so I went to pick her up and carried her to the other side of the house.

Then the cops said something and went in my door as if they didn't want me to take my daughter to the other side of the house where the living room is. I got loud and told him something along with recording them and letting him know I will talk to and hold my daughter. I also asked, "Are you married?" and he said yes. I said how would you like it if your wife cheated on you and took the kids. They kept quiet. I state now let me talk to my kids. They backed from the door and just waited.

Our oldest daughter left with her, and I was very upset. I told her that if you leave your house for a woman who disrespected your dad by having an affair with a married man, then I will not forgive you. While the cops were here, she was packing the car. My wife and daughter left with their things. She hired movers who came shortly after and didn't pay them. I helped them move her things into the truck and later paid them for the service after he told me she never paid him.

Trying to leave with our kids after neglecting them for a married man out of state was the cherry on top. While she was flying back, she texted, saying all the kids would be with her. I just could not believe it, she got caught cheating, and was going to commit suicide after being caught, and she wants to take all the kids out of their family home. It's not like she has anywhere to go. She manipulates those kids so much, they don't even know it. Hell, she manipulated me so much, and I didn't see it either.

I cannot blame my kids for wanting to go with her after the lies she tells. My oldest son Jaiden told her no, he was staying. My other two sons eventually stayed with me. I know her thoughts went along the lines of taking the kids so she could get more child support, food stamps, and some type of housing assistance.

She loves using people and taking advantage of the system to benefit her. The more kids, the better the chances of resources. Since her plan did not work, now she needs me and her parents to help her survive. She was trying to get rid of all of us.

The next day I called James' wife again. I asked her where he was on a specific day in the summer. She said he was out with his line brothers. I told her that my wife flew out of state to go not far from your area and was at the casino alone on that day. She told me they got into a big fight, and he came back home around five in the morning that night. She got loud on the phone and said, "Oh my God." It all made sense; they were together.

In one of his messages, he said when are you coming back to Lake Mason, she said in a few months. Then they continued with messages like, you enjoyed making out with me, etc. This confirmed that they slept together when she went to the casino, since he was gone that entire night as well per his wife. Now, what are the odds of that! I was angry that she put my daughter at risk, as I know she slept with a married man in the summer when she went out there with her mom for a gathering.

After realizing my baby girl's health was at risk along with mine, I immediately panicked. My wife slept with a married man. I am sure if he is sleeping with her from states away, he is also sleeping with other people in his state. I went to the doctor to get tested for sexually transmitted diseases and HIV. I also got my daughter tested to make sure she was safe from any sexually transmitted diseases, as her mother was breastfeeding her at the time of her affair. I then requested that my wife get tested as well for any STDs and HIV.

If a married man is cheating on his wife with a married woman states away, what makes her think he is not cheating on his wife with other women in his area? I have never in my life wanted to call a woman out of her name, but clearly this one desires the name. The only reason I haven't called it like it is, is because I'm a man of God. So, just imagine the frustration and know that the same words that come to your mind; those are my thoughts exactly.

I guess she wasn't thinking about that, since she was in love. Even though I never wanted to leave my wife or have sex with someone, I would never put my wife and daughter at risk. Imagine I sleep with someone and get a sexually transmitted disease, then give it to my wife, then my daughter is breastfed, and then she gets it.

These messages disgusted me to my bones. I could not believe my wife, who I knew since high school, a virtuous God-fearing woman, the mother of my five kids, the woman I wanted to spend the rest of my life with, the woman I trust and love, the woman I would die for was doing this. I could not even imagine myself sending naked pictures of myself to a married woman and she is sending naked pictures of herself to a married man. We both plan to use our current spouses, plan the great escape, leave our marriages, and later get married. I could not imagine trying to destroy my kids' family home with both parents active in their lives.

Since Leslie's plan did not work, she moved to a hotel, then three Airbnb's over the span of a month. Then she started staying in one Airbnb each month until she could move into an apartment. She ends up having to move in that "trashy area" her words, she did not like where I dropped her parents at.

My daughter decided she would now visit me on the weekends, giving me 1.5 days of the week with her. I tried to talk to her the first two weekends she came to visit and just nothing. I apologized to her for saying I wasn't going to forgive her. I was mad at the time. Imagine you sacrifice your entire life for your wife and kids, and they all decide to leave you. Even when you've done nothing wrong. She destroyed her entire family, yet you get punished for it.

This is what she wants, so she has the right to decide where she wants to live and for how long she wants to go. In most states, kids the age of 14 can stay with whom they want, even if you fight for joint or full custody over them as long as there are no other issues that warrant otherwise. I had to deal with this, losing my daughter who stayed with me for most of her childhood. It also hurt my feelings that her mother would not tell her to spend half the time with her dad and to be with her little sister, especially since I funded everything she did and supported her dance classes and out of state trips. I would drop Lauren to dance class and pick her up from dance class three times a week. In addition to dropping her to school and picking her up from school. Now, I will never have this experience.

Her mother spoiled her a lot by buying her food throughout the week, even when Leslie's mother cooked. Her mom would always buy fast foods as well. Now, many times Lauren comes with fast food on Fridays when she comes visit us. The older kids are just looking as to say why didn't my mom buy us food as well. I feel so bad for them when the mom buys fast food for the one child and not the others.

Now, my two daughters barely see each other. My youngest daughter is with me throughout the week.

My little girl Ilana always says when Lauren coming. It breaks my heart every time she says something about wanting to spend time with Lauren. I do get her for like 1-2 hours on a Saturday once a month so I can have all five of the kids just for a little while so they can spend time with each other. This just crush my spirit every time as I never have all five kids at the same time beside the 1-2 hours a month.

Still, beneath the pain, another instinct surfaced, the need to protect my children. Whatever storm was gathering between their mother and me, they deserved stability. They deserved a father who remained steady even when his world trembled.

Faith, the anchor I had relied on for years, now felt both comforting and challenging. I repeated scripture not out of habit but out of necessity, searching for ground that would hold me. Strength, I realized, was no longer about silence alone. It was about endurance without losing myself.

In quiet moments, a sobering truth emerged, the marriage I believed I was safeguarding had been changing long before I recognized it. The discovery did not create the fracture; it revealed one that had already formed.

And as I sat with that realization, I understood something else, this was only the beginning of a reckoning that would reshape everything I thought I knew about love, trust, and the life we had built together.

CHAPTER 7

REACTIONS AND REVELATIONS

I learned something unsettling in the weeks that followed. Silence can be louder than confrontation. Leslie's future husband stopped talking to her. According to her, he chose to remain with his wife and pursue counseling. Just like that, the future she had been building behind my back disappeared. He was never going to leave his wife and kids in Texas to move to Los Angeles for someone with five kids and two parents to take care of.

She already had plans to remarry and told me, yes, I was going to marry him, but we decided to squash that. You cannot play with people's lives like this. And just because your plan didn't work, you cannot use me as your backup. I will never again allow one person in my life to use me again. I am guarding my heart because I will not allow one family member close enough for them to hurt me and mess up my mental health again.

He ran to the church as well, just like my separated wife did. Amazing how they run to God to ask forgiveness so fast after spending months of deceiving their family, but in the previous days, they were talking about having sex with each other, planning to get married, and loving one another. They both knew exactly what they were doing and were playing a dangerous game.

In a matter of weeks, she lost both the man she was preparing to leave me for and the marriage she had already fractured. It's not like she didn't know these things already. She is a smart woman, well at least I thought, have multiple degrees and was in the top of her class and should know better than having an affair.

However, she was planning to move out there around Lake Mason. My mom told me Leslie stated she will eventually move around Lake Mason, Texas. I assume she was going to move there for him. Which means she was going to leave all five of her kids for a married man because she cannot leave the state with our kids.

One evening, I found myself standing in the kitchen watching her move casually between the refrigerator and the counter, as if our lives were not lying in pieces around us. The hum of the appliance filled the silence neither of us seemed ready to break.

"How did we get here?" I wondered, studying her face for traces of the woman I married. She looked familiar, yet strangely distant, like someone I used to know.

Grief does not always arrive as a wave. Sometimes it settles slowly, like dust after a collapse. I was not only mourning my marriage. I was mourning the future I believed was secure, the trust I had carried without question, the identity I held as a husband who thought his home was safe.

Revelation is supposed to bring clarity. Instead, it felt like standing inside a house that was collapsing in slow motion, each beam cracking one after another while I tried to remain upright beneath the weight.

Yet I could not ignore the bitter irony. People who had spent months deceiving their families suddenly ran toward faith once they were exposed. It forced me to wrestle with a difficult question, how do people compartmentalize wrongdoing so completely, only to seek mercy when the consequences arrive?

The answer never came. Instead, I began writing letters.

After my father died, I realized you never asked if I was okay. Not once. you have not shown me much sympathy, compassion, love, or care. You did not ask what I needed or how you could support me. You just went on with your life.

Putting the words down felt less like accusation and more like documentation. I needed a record. Something steady to hold onto when my memory began questioning itself. I wrote about the distance that had crept into our conversations. About the way she lingered on her phone. About how even small exchanges now felt strained, as if we were strangers attempting politeness.

I wrote about exhaustion, the kind that settles into your bones after years of carrying responsibility without relief. I had worked multiple jobs for so long that fatigue felt normal. I told her plainly in the letter: my body is tired. No one should have to live like this.

On October 8, 2024, I asked you how your day was, and you said it was good. I was trying to start a conversation. You didn't say much, nor did you ask how my day was, especially after you knew I'd driven about four hours. I said I almost fell asleep, so I got an energy drink.

Your response was, you slept all night, why are you tired? Interesting comment. I feel like I cannot say much to you anymore.

You never told me anything about the rental price, or anything. You left without saying anything while I was working in the shed, and you never texted. I made sure to go out to kiss you and say, "Have a good day," on October 8th.

My credit cards are all maxed out with a bunch of food purchases and take outs. Why is this? You should be helping me with my credit since yours is not good, and you are not really working on it. I have been telling you that I am trying to build wealth, and you are not trying to do the same for the family.

I am tired of working multiple jobs and getting nowhere with my income, savings, and trying to establish generational wealth. I do not even know what you do with your income; it appears I pay for everything. Especially when we spent almost $25,000 in the month of September.

When I looked at the bank account for the previous month, we had spent a ridiculous amount of money. I told her that we have been having budgeting issues for years, and now I am taking control of everything to ensure we budget correctly. We sat down, went over every bill, and created an Excel sheet that works. To do this, we need to look at previous months' spending and enter it in the Excel sheet. What she was somewhat using from time to time never matched and was off by thousands from what we spent.

What unsettled me most was not only the affair itself, but the realization that cracks had existed long before I recognized them. Financial strain, emotional distance, and conversations avoided. Respect slowly eroding in ways I had minimized. Had I mistaken endurance for strength?

The memory remains painfully vivid. When I discovered more messages, my body reacted before my mind could process them. My hands trembled. My stomach tightened until I thought I might be sick. I tried to stand and had to steady myself against the desk. The love of my life was sharing herself with another married man. I remember whispering aloud, "This cannot be real." But it was.

What unsettled me even more was how ordinary everything appeared around us. The children still laughed down the hallway. The television played somewhere in the background. Life, indifferent to my devastation, continued moving forward. It was hard knowing that I was living my own reality in the mist of my family's.

Later in the evening while I laid in bed, I stared at the ceiling replaying every year of our marriage, searching for signs I might have overlooked. Moments once harmless now felt suspicious under this new light. By morning, I understood something I had never fully grasped before: Betrayal rarely begins with one decision. It is usually the result of many small permissions given over time.

October 10th, I went to the restroom, and you said quickly, "I am pooping. What do you want?" The tone was off, and you moved your hand swiftly, which is not the first time I saw this while you were using the restroom. Something is off, perhaps you are constipated. You did come into the shed and I said have a good day, love you.

That same night is when I saw all the messages and sexting, explicit messages and images sent from you to James and from James to you. I was sick to my stomach, I could not eat, I was weak, throwing up and nothing coming out. I could not believe my eyes on what I was reading. To know the love of my life is having an affair with another married man. I would never in my life cheat on you.

As the letters continue, many times I was just praying and asking God to reveal what Leslie was hiding from me. I needed to know everything about her relationship with James. Most of my reasoning was because of the kids that were involved because it wasn't just our kids, but James' as well. Maybe they would care a bit more for the kids since they clearly didn't care about me.

I wrote about how much you changed. Less affection. You started telling your parents you loved them more and less when it came to me. I'm sure James was also being told that you loved him more than me. God revealed to me that you were telling him. Funny thing is, Leslie was the one who said, "Once a cheater, always a cheater." There was also a time she said, "How he gets you is how he will lose you."

In another letter, I wrote about the years I spent trying to build stability for our family. The long hours. The sacrifices. The belief that if I worked hard enough, our children would inherit something stronger than what we started with. I had dreamed of generational wealth, of giving them opportunities I never had. Yet somewhere along the way, survival replaced vision.

"I just wanted a normal life," I wrote. Not luxury, not excess, just partnership. Just the feeling that I was not carrying everything alone. Los Angeles was expensive, yes, but the deeper cost was invisible measured in stress, fatigue, and the quiet fear that no matter how much I worked, it would never be enough. Still, I never imagined betrayal would enter our story.

One night, while rereading what I had written, a childhood memory surfaced with startling clarity. I grew up with my dad committing adultery it was not cool. So as an adult I find it to be the worst thing you can do to someone and Leslie knows that. I caught my dad cheating at the age of six with another woman. My mom left him after that.

I knew then and growing up I promised myself that when I married, I would build something different. Something faithful. And for years, I believed I had.

Realizing my children might now experience a similar fracture broke something deep inside me. The pain was no longer mine alone. I cannot stop crying, stressing, and praying daily for them. Leslie hurt me to my soul, I cannot imagine ever doing this to her. Did she really want to neglect her family for another man?

In the quiet after midnight, one thought returned repeatedly, was any of it real? The anniversary celebrations. The notes, the affection, and the reassurances that we were strong. Had she already been preparing to leave while asking if I would spend the rest of my life with her? I searched her recent kindness for authenticity and found myself afraid of the answer.

For most of my life, I believed being strong meant absorbing pain without complaint. Providing without pause. Enduring without acknowledgment. Now I began to question whether silence had protected my marriage or slowly buried it. Strength, I was learning, is not always quiet endurance. Sometimes it is the courage to face what you never wanted to see. Sometimes it is telling the truth, even when that truth rearranges your entire life.

In the days ahead, more conversations would come. More truths would surface. Decisions would have to be made, the kind that divide a life into before and after. But standing there in the wreckage of what I thought was permanent, I understood one thing with unsettling certainty.

The betrayal was no longer hidden. And nothing about my life would ever be the same again.

Once I finished processing my true emotions with everything. I took time to read all the letters that I planned to send. I sent them all while I was at work so that I had nothing to distract me or talk me out of it. It was time for everyone to know that I was aware of their involvement. I needed them to know how much they hurt me. It didn't matter if they responded or not.

```
Hello Alisha (wife best friend),
```

I hope you are doing well and in good spirits.

It saddens me to know that you knew my wife was cheating on me and planning on leaving me to be with a married man. She has been talking to you a lot lately and for long periods of time. I have evidence of all the text and calls during instructional hours while you and my wife were supposed to be working. I am grieving the recent loss of my 63-year-old dad (you knew this and came to the funeral) and you knew my wife was sleeping with another man at the same time.

You should be ashamed of yourself for supporting a married woman of 18 years to cheat on me and plans on leaving me next year. You even helped her pay for some of the homecoming travel knowing what she was going to do. What kind of woman are you? This is not a Godly woman. You should have prayed and supported your friend the right way. I never cheated on Leslie, and you saw I gave her everything.

You and your husband Tony have problems and you always share with Leslie. You put up with Tony and are still married to him, but it makes me wonder what you are doing. Perhaps you are also cheating on your husband since you support that behavior.

Since you support her so much, now you can help her with her current situation.

Sincerely,

Heartbroken Grieving Husband

Tony is my wife's best friend's husband. After speaking with him, he said I blocked your wife years ago after she was talking bad about you to my wife while she was also talking about me.

Hello Tony,

I hope all is well.

I just found out Leslie is cheating on me with a married man who lives in Texas. Your wife Alisha knew this. I am so heartbroken she supported this behavior. I am not sure if you knew this as well as I was blind. Below is a message I sent your wife.

Sincerely,

Heartbroken Grieving Husband

Dear James,

You have caused so much pain and suffering for my family. You are sleeping with my married wife, and you are a married man. We have been married for 18 years and now it is over. Why get married if you want to cheat? As a man, would you have liked it if your wife did that to you and took your kids away from you? I really want you to think about that. I am so hurt that you would do this to your wife and my family.

I am still grieving the loss of my dad as you already know that, although I did not get a chance to really grieve because all this just happened. Both of you were texting the day of my dad's funeral and while I was back and forth in Texas to care for my dying dad. You should be better than that James. She even sent you the video of her singing and I still never received it, that is evil.

I pulled all the evidence from my family AT&T account which shows all the text messages and hours of phone calls during work hours. How were both of you able to pull that off? She works with kids at school and you're sending sexual messages while kids are present in the classroom. You sent her naked pictures of yourself during her instructional hours and while you were supposed to be working. You guys hid this so well, so I am sure the kids did not see the text message and the Instagram pictures you sent her that deletes after she sees it. You found time to travel to meet up with my wife during company hours and sleep with my wife.

You slept with my wife when she went to Texas during the times of August 1st - 3rd. When she went to the SunStar World Casino on Sunday. I have the proof.

You neglect your family as a husband to go sleep with another man's wife. This is beyond disgusting. My wife said Alisha wants to go to our university homecoming, so she is going to go. I found it strange that my dad was in hospice care at the time, and she is thinking about homecoming. She went out there to sleep with you.

The kids suffer at this point. I never wanted to cheat on my wife because I saw what that did to me catching my dad in bed with another woman at the age of six. I never wanted my kids to grow up in a single-family home. I have filed for divorce.

It also hurts that as my Fraternity brother; you should know better and should have respect the brotherhood. I also helped bring you in and never had nothing bad to say about you.

I am praying for your wife Erika and your two kids. You have caused extreme pain in my life, marriage, and my five kids. They will never forget what you and my wife did to our family. I am informing my kids on what both of you did to them. I hope your wife does the same.

Please come and pick up my wife Leslie Wint now. You can have her and be married after my divorce and your divorce is final.

After I emailed my fraternity brother, there was no response. Not even an acknowledgment. The silence said more than any apology could have. In that quiet, I realized something important, I did not need revenge. Justice did not belong to me. "Vengeance is mine, says the Lord." I repeated the scripture not as performance, but as survival.

Other letters from past years to my wife.

Hello Leslie,

I have concluded and confirmed that you don't want me to do anything without you. After I am with you 95% of the time. Even your mother notices this. The first time I went to watch the football game this season, she even stated he wanted to go watch it by himself.

You stated in a negative tone, why can't you watch it here, I purchased the package (so you want me to just sit at home to watch all the games). I cannot even do that because your mother is always in the seat I sit in, but it is HER SEAT. I then watch some games in the room, so I don't have to fight for a seat in my own house. No need to bother her, I will watch all the TV in the room, so I do not need her seat. The time I watched it at home, you have an attitude stating we don't want to watch the game all day. All throughout the season, you had a problem if I went to watch the game at Dave and Busters. I only went twice without you. There is a problem when I go and another when I stay at home.

After working over 50 hours weekly, you continue to try and control me and not appreciate the stuff I do for "7" people in the house, not even myself. I work all these jobs and still can't see or do anything with the money as it goes to all the bills. I am still applying for jobs and for us to enjoy life. I am tired of continuing to work my ass off and just pay bills. Then you have a problem when I go out and drink.

The worst weekend was Dec. 1st., I was working and got off at 6p.m. You were going to Ms. Kathy (which took you almost three hours including driving). I stayed to work later talking to a customer, Nor, and then Miley since you always timing me (you made a comment, you got off at 6). Then you called me, and I told you I went to Dave and Busters for a drink. Since you were already going to do her make up, you would have probably been back at 9p.m. if you went as planned. Then you asked who am I with, why do I have to be with someone? Why can't I go anywhere by myself?

Why can't I get a break to just hangout by myself and watch a game, a fight, or just get 1-2 drinks?

Why are you with someone you cannot trust? Why are you insecure?

You then made a big deal about that talking about you saying you wanted to spend time with kids. And probably talking bad about me in front of them. Yet, you steadily bring up this incident after a drink from work to Dave and Busters, when you were going to do her hair. I told the kids we can go to the movies and I was coming back. I made it at like eight something and had plenty of time to get dressed and make it to the movies on time. I still spent time with them but couldn't really enjoy it because of your behavior. Again, you are still not satisfied or appreciative.

I work so many weeks and NEVER see them, yet you do not give a damn about that as you NEVER tell them to call me and say good night. I am rushing home to wake them up to tell them goodnight. But let me go on a trip or somewhere overnight, you will fuss and say you never called us. Interesting!

The very next day, Saturday, I went to watch the football game at Dave and Busters. Again, attitude questioning, "Who you with". Again, why do I have to be with someone? Then you even drive there to just see if I was there and if I'm with someone. Then hang up on me. How can you think this is a life I like with you doing this? How are you okay with even doing all of this?

I was going to Colorado with Line Brothers/Kevin 1.5 years ago, I cancelled because I was going to spend time with you. Also, you still did not want me to go. Why are you still going if they cancelled you asked, yet you know Lorenzo lives there as well. Why couldn't you set up a trip for me afterwards to cancel to be with you? I will answer that, you NEVER thought about that.

We have been dealing with the same things for years. I am tired of not being able to go anywhere, especially when it's down the street to watch a game. You stay trying to listen to my conversations on the phone, to know everything I say and do. Even at the other house, Jerad and Jonah saw you listening, including myself. Yet, we were just talking, nothing crazy or bad. One time you had a big issue in front of my company for spitting on the damn ground, I was so embarrassed. Yet, your dad is steadily burning all our patio furniture with his cigarettes, yet you say NOTHING to him.

I do not know any woman who has the time for all this and why would they do this to a hard-working husband.

You are mean/negative to me many times and show so much negativity and sometimes hate in front of kids. I try to be nice to you and treat you well despite all of this. Like at the movies, you screamed at me and were mean. When I tell you something you don't like, you're quick to attack.

You may ask, if I am happy. The answer is I am not and have not been for a while with a lot of these things. I especially do not like how you talk to me and treat me like I am your kid. Hiding stuff from me, for example alcohol. You do not allow me to be a man many times. You do what you want (mainly with the funds) and I don't question you. We have yet to have a budget. I work three full time jobs and still can't make it, yet you sweat me for going to Dave and Buster.

I do not think you appreciate what I do (and how good you have it), from supporting your parents (they could never make it on their own, nor can you afford to take care of them alone), from paying over 10,000 for you to look good, over 10, 000 for you to do insurance and that first one failed, from paying over $20,000 for your own agency, from paying majority of the bills (many married women I know pay about half the bills or closer).

You have it good and better than most women. You went years without working while I still held it down.

You bust through the door one day, when I am at home watching porn. You were mad and had a problem. For what???? I cannot even play with my damn self, which is normal. That was really horrible. Yet, you can pleasure yourself with a vibrator with me and without me. One night you did, I woke up. I never said a word, why should I get mad for that.

We are in a new year, and you will not control me anymore. I will go out without you and you will have to be okay with it. I am tired of living how you want me to live (work my life away, make all the money, spend time only with you, the kids, and your parents only).

In closing, yes, I love you. Sincerely,

Your Loving Husband.

I wrote the above weeks ago. Below is a continuation. I just do not know when I will send this letter. I stopped after day three.

Other Notes/Messages Sent to Wife in Previous Years

January 1, 2021

As soon as I went upstairs, you snuck up on me by the door (not sure if you thought I was on the phone), but said you needed a restroom. It appears every time I go up, you come up. But maybe I am overthinking that part.

January 2, 2021

You called me right after I left home (you noticed from the ring I left). When I answered the phone, you asked where I was going with no hesitation. I said going to the gym. I think you felt guilty because you said, I heard music, so I wasn't sure where you were.

January 3, 2021

You text, have you gotten here yet? When asked, get where, you never responded. I just made it to the gym, so I am assuming you wanted to know where I was.

Later that night, I came in to tell everybody hi, give you a kiss. I said nice cake, but I cannot eat it because it has too much sugar. Instead of being happy and trying to support me, you said, "that means no alcohol", in front of kids. Again negative, no positive from you. You make it seem like I have a problem with alcohol when I am always at the house or with you somewhere. I am not going to address why the kids were present watching a file language movie, but no biggie.

FYI: You have a good man, one who is not interested in other women, not cheating on you, loves you and is in love with you, but you are steadily pushing me away.

On. Aug. 18 you brought up another married man, who had an interest in your art, while we were watching a movie and having a good night. I had already talked to you about the flip and assume you notice I was down, but you still brought up a conversation that also brought me down.

You said the man from PVU asked if it was okay to talk on the phone. I am assuming he knows you and already feels comfortable with you through chat communication to ask that. You said how would your wife feel. To me, this means you want to talk to him and see what he has to say. Otherwise, you would have said, I am happily married to a hard-working husband who supports and takes care of me.

I cannot talk to a married man over the phone. I probably would have kissed you and really respected you.

This is another way of showing me, you do not respect me at all. You do not care that I pay all the bills, taking care of the kids, you, and your parents.

I bust my ass working six jobs to pay bills, still do not have much to show, trying hard to add more income and not more expenses, only one trying to do this.

Back to the point, he said that his wife does not go through his phone and he does not go through hers. You said your phone is open, so it does not matter. You guys had a conversation about phones, I am sure you said my husband's phone is locked, etc…you left that part out.

Then both of you talked about cheating as a subject. This entails both of you having it on your mind or trying to start something. It appears if he caught his wife, it would not be a big deal. This tells me he cheated on his wife before and tried to seduce you. You said if my husband cheats, I will do it to get back at him. Like why would you even do that, say that to another married man who obviously likes/wants you, and then say that to me.

This is not the first time you communicated with a married man. Years ago, you were texting James while we were watching a movie. I never said a word, until this letter.

Also, your dad is constantly stinking up the house and it is like a joke to you. That is nasty, I do not want to even be in my own house, the kitchen and living room. I am sweating my ass off in the shed but that's my only option.

I remembered you scream at me in front of my company who spit from the balcony. Spit that leaves the ground. She had an attitude and problem. After that I never had anyone else over, beside Hason. I will not invite any over as well. I caught you multiple times listening to me on the phone and with company at the house. Jerad and Jonah saw you listening to us at the Lancaster House, no privacy.

In closing, I do not entertain any woman who I know trying to get with me. As soon as you open up that type of Pandora's Box, you know what comes out of it.

This was another level of disrespect towards me. However, you have no issues doing that.

You saw, I did not say a word about that/responded. I stayed watching the movie we were watching and playing with Ilana, while trying to control my thoughts.

You went to bed. Did not kiss me good night, and did not give a damn about my feelings.

To a man who gives you all, pays ALL the bills, works his ass off.

One day, I will get enough.

Writing on Friday, September 8, 2023

This past week you have again not shown respect.

On Sunday, August 20th, you scream at me. Which you do this a lot.

Many nights you go to bed and do not tell me good night, or you love me. I love you so much, but you have pushed me away through the years.

Sharing Respect Letter

To: Leslie · Thu, Sep 7, 2023 at 12:15 AM

Hello,

I am just sharing one of the letters to myself while I am being very open with you. You should respect that I am sharing this, and this is how I felt typing it at that time.

There was another long one from last year, but it's gone with the other computer.

You dd not like my recent letter to make things right. You should be glad I am telling you how I feel. After a while, a man will stop writing letters to himself and cheat or move on.

This is another thing, I cannot communicate with you, I cannot express myself. So, I have to write it down. Then, when I share it, it is a hate letter. To live a life not saying shit because your wife thinks it's a hate letter, etc. or not to hurt her is not the way to go for the rest of your life.

As of today, I do not know what I really want to do. Just understand that please.

Yes, I love you.

On Aug. 21st you said Goodnight Will, love you and went to his room. You did not tell me a word. I show you so much love and respect and you give none back.

I am very unhappy in our marriage, and I cannot fix you nor can you fix me. We may need to just co-parent.

If I was a woman and my husband is taking care of me, my parents and all the kids. I would make sure he is happy. I would not disrespect or ever get loud with him. You do not even suck my dick, maybe 1-2 times this 2023 year, that is crazy. I talked to two married men for years of marriage and they were like what, that is crazy. You never initiate sex nor even care to have sex, jack me off, or suck my dick. I have never cheated on you. I am very lonely here. I feel alone all the time. I love the kids, but I do not want to be in this marriage anymore. I want to be happy and I really think that is not being married.

I cannot even enjoy the house I pay all the bills for. I sweat in the shed. Your mother hogs the TV, then she's like you can have it. I just decided to go upstairs. So, I can only watch after she goes upstairs at 6 PM. Your dad is stinking the entire kitchen up, I gag in there. This is just depressing.

I can recall when you screamed at me and embarrassed me in front of my friends for one of them spitting from the balcony. You do not want me to have any friends, since you do not have any friends out here. Also, you do not want me to do anything or go anywhere. I have enough of this. I do not want anyone telling me what to do or to go. I do not want to answer to anyone.

I am constantly stressing over here, and you keep having the account go negative with $35 fees. It is stressful that all these years of marriage we have yet to manage our money right. I am killing myself working here trying to provide for nine people.

I wish I had it as easy as you. I wish someone would love and respect me and show it. I wish I wouldn't have to work so hard to survive. I wish I could just work 1 job to live. I wish my life was not so difficult and hard. I am tired and exhausted. I cannot fight for our marriage as I feel it is coming to an end.

I reached out to my kid's school informing them and to check on my kids during this traumatic experience.

Hello Dell Academy Team,

I hope all is well.

I recently caught my wife, Leslie, cheating on me with a married man out of state and was preparing to leave me next year before I go on a work trip next summer out of the county and marry him after he divorce his wife. This all occurred while my daddy was in hospice and died. This is tragic for Leslie to do this to a person, this is very evil. She has brought extreme pain on the family and now we are divided. I am having a hard time dealing with this.

Darien is staying with me in our house. Please keep an eye out for him at school to make sure he is okay, perhaps a counselor can also reach out to him. I will drop him off and pick him up every day.

Please share with his other teachers to check up on him, I do not have all the emails. Thank you,

After sending this email to the principal and other teachers, two of the teachers reached out to provide support and check on my son.

One of the middle school teachers, not on the email, heard what happened and asked if I was happier now. I could not believe she would say such a thing after I dropped my son off at school.

Hello Mrs. Cara,

I thought I added you to the email. To answer your question, I'm not happy. Leslie hurt me to the core, and you should know that. She wasted 18 years of my life to cheat on a man that supported her and her parents, the other man was married. This is the ultimate betrayer. I wish this on no married couple. The Bible says do not commit adultery. Leslie is an evil spirited woman and God will handle her for causing me so much pain and suffering and now my kids are suffering because of her. I cannot sleep at night because of all this. It hurts!!

Please pray for my kids and I. Leslie is not who you think she is. Don't let her tell you lies about how she cheated to make me happy. That makes no sense.

How would she have liked me to say, "Are you happy about leaving your kids to go to another country with a new man while your kids are with their father in another country and you can barely see them. Are you happy with leaving your kids behind and starting a new life?" I bet she would not like that response.

This goes to say people think they can say whatever they want to someone and then as soon as someone gives them a taste of their own medicine, they automatically become the victim. Interesting how people can be!

I know my tone could have improved on the letters, but when you are betrayed by the people you know, tone typically do not come off the best way.

CHAPTER 8

FAMILY FRACTURES

L eslie wanted her parents to go to a nursing home. Her dad didn't believe me, so I showed him the message from her regarding putting them in assisted living. Her father leaned in, read the words slowly, and the shift in his breathing was immediate. He did not explode or argue; instead, he grew still in a way that spoke louder than anger.

After a long silence, he simply repeated that he was not going anywhere. Leslie's dad stood firm in the living room, his posture rigid and his voice unwavering. He told me plainly that he was not going to a nursing home. There was no hesitation in his tone, only resolve. Leslie's mother lingered nearby, quiet but visibly unsettled, her eyes moving between us as if she sensed something heavy was about to surface.

Leslie was not going to allow her parents to mess up and interrupt her new marriage. She did not care for her parents living with us because of how they were. The betrayal had already fractured our home, but it also exposed patterns that had existed long before the affair. Leslie's parents argued constantly, often in front of the children, their words sharp and careless. Her father would curse at her mother without restraint.

My three-year-old daughter would repeat the awful words Leslie's dad would say and when I would hear this, I would get upset. When I asked where she had learned it, she pointed toward the kitchen at her grandfather. My heart sank. I spoke with Leslie about this on several occasions and said that was not okay.

The children were absorbing everything they heard. She brushed it off casually, saying that was just how her parents were as they got older. I could not help but notice that if the roles had been reversed and it were my parents behaving that way, the response would have been immediate and firm. But since it was her parents, she let it slide and laughed it off. I learned to swallow my frustration and grow quieter, convincing myself that keeping the peace was strength.

Less than two months from the separation, Leslie's father died of a heart attack. When I received the news, I did not feel vindicated or justified. I felt sick. A friend asked whether I thought everything that had happened contributed to his death, and though I could not prove it medically, I knew stress changes a person. The upheaval, the betrayal, the uncertainty, none of it leaves the heart untouched. My kids lost both of their grandfathers in two months.

Children carry grief differently. Sometimes it appears as silence, other times as unexpected anger or forced laughter. As I watched them navigate emotions, they were too young to fully understand, I realized that I was no longer dealing only with betrayal. I was living inside its consequences.

Many of my family members are negative and gossip about other family members. I do not want to be involved with anyone who speaks negatively about any family member then talks to them like nothing is going on. As the voice on the other end began offering opinions about the situation, I interrupted and said I did not want to hear anything negative about anyone. When they tried to continue, I ended the call. The silence afterward felt cleaner than the conversation ever could have.

Talking on the phone is a waste of my time if you are not uplifting, motivating, trying to support, being positive, or praying with someone. I refuse to continue a generation of curses that will make me bitter and have negative energy. I pray to God to remove any negative person or energy out of my life, and I do not care who they are.

If anyone is not for me God, please remove them immediately. God also gives us the discernment to detach ourselves from such people as well. It becomes difficult when it is your own family members, friends, and some church members. One may feel as if I need to respect them, but one must have the ultimate self-respect from themselves and not allow someone's actions to make you feel some type of way. You should never tolerate a person just because they are family.

Some family members are meant to just pass through our life and not part of our life journey and that is okay. You can also love from a distance and not carry the burden of being forced to deal with people. Many family members would never be friends; however, we just deal with them and say well that's how such and such is or you know how those Scorpios and Libras are, etc. We let outside forces dictate how we should act and then let that determine who you are and should become. One must be strong in God and read the Bible on how we should treat people and act and lead us not into temptation but deliver us from the evil one.

I thought everyone knew and said this prayer daily. Interesting how it is not applied in many daily lives, but they say it. Just like people say I will pray for you, or I care, yet the actions do not show it. You can say and recite all these words, but if no action is evident, none of those things matters. If I thought the betrayal stopped with her and him, I was wrong.

When I finally shared the truth with my family, I expected shock or grief. Instead, I encountered reactions that cut deeper than I anticipated. Some offered genuine comfort, and their quiet support carried me through days when breathing itself felt heavy. Others minimized what had happened. They reminded me she was still the mother of my children, as if biology could soften the impact of betrayal.

Some called it a mistake and encouraged me to move on. But this was not a mistake. It was a deliberate choice, repeated and hidden. What hurt most were the subtle shifts in loyalty. I was told she felt lonely, that I worked too much, that perhaps I had not been emotionally present. Hearing that felt like being wounded all over again. I had worked tirelessly to provide stability, to build a future, and to hold our family together. Now my sacrifice was being reframed as neglect.

The realization deepened when I learned that my brother and his wife had sent Leslie nearly a thousand dollars within a day of me informing them about what had happened. No one called to ask how I was managing. No one asked what I needed. Soon after, I saw church members and relatives supporting her financially as well.

A social media content creator shares a post that a homeless single mother of five needed support. Leslie had done created a go fund me post. I later found out those funding was going to a hotel for her to stay at for Lauren competition that was an hour away.

Meanwhile, I was struggling to maintain the household and meet responsibilities that once felt manageable. Observing how easily sympathy flowed toward her while I quietly carried the financial and emotional weight forced me to confront another difficult truth, some people support the version of events that feels most comfortable to them, even when it ignores reality.

Through all of this, my faith began to change shape. I had always believed strength meant endurance, prayer, and holding everything together without breaking. Now my prayers sounded different. I asked God to remove anyone from my life who was not meant to walk beside me, regardless of who they were. Discernment became less of an abstract spiritual idea and more of a daily necessity. It guided me toward protecting my peace, toward loving certain people from a distance rather than allowing their presence to reopen wounds.

Late one night, after the house had grown quiet and the children were asleep, I sat alone reflecting on everything the betrayal had uncovered. It was not only my marriage that had fractured; it was the illusion that family loyalty was automatic and unshakable. I saw how dysfunction can travel through generations when no one chooses to confront it. I saw how easily people normalize harmful behavior with phrases meant to excuse rather than correct. In that stillness, I made a promise to myself that the cycle would end with me. Not the pain, and not the memories, but the acceptance of patterns that destroy rather than heal.

If I had once believed the betrayal was confined to two people, I understood now that it rippled outward, revealing truths I might never have faced otherwise. Yet within that painful clarity came a quieter realization that strength is not pretending the wound does not exist. Strength is acknowledging it, learning from it, and deciding that what broke you will not define what comes next.

CHAPTER 9

WHEN NO ONE ANSWERED

I mailed family Christmas pictures. My mom received her pictures first and told me thank you so much and they were really nice. I mailed Christmas cards to my uncle, aunts, brothers, and sisters, and no one thanked me. My dad's fiancée delivered it and thanked me for the pictures, saying they were very nice. I asked my aunt and brother if they received the mail I sent weeks ago; my aunt said yes, it's on the fridge, she never said thank you for the pictures came out nice. I had to bring it up. My brother stated he hadn't checked his mail in two weeks and never thanked me when he did receive it.

After taking time out of my busy schedule to write on each picture and handwrite on the envelope, I mailed it, and I cannot even get a thank-you text or anything. Other siblings never said thank you or that the pictures looked good, not a word. I called another aunt's phone, left a message, and she never called me back.

These are the actions I will remember. I am not ever mailing them a single picture again. Why do I have to keep chasing people to love, support, respond, and care for me? Family and friends did not constantly check up on me to see if I was okay mentally, or just to send a prayer or words of encouragement consistently. Not one person offered anything financially to see if I needed it. However, this was offered and given to my ex by my family members.

I had a close friend say, "Would you like the phone number for two other men who helped me when my wife cheated on me while going through a divorce". I was like really; you are my friend and experience this. I also was there for him when his wife did this. Yet, he was throwing me to strangers who helped him. I would rather it be my friend.

Feeling betrayed by your family and not supported was one of the most hurtful, disappointing things in my life besides losing a child, my dad, and my wife. Remember, God does not sleep. He sees and hears everything that people are doing to you. No weapon formed against you shall prosper. God will not allow others to harm you. Also, remember, vengeance is mine, says the lord.

Let him fight the evil that stands against you; their day will come. They all felt sorry for Leslie. My family even called and comforted her. They continued to tell me to find it in my heart to forgive her and take her back. My mom said to take her back multiple times. After my grandmother kept calling me, I would not answer.

I finally called her back, and she said the same thing that my aunts, uncle, and mother said. I told her not to pray for me to take her back, as God revealed this to me because I asked God, and it was not to take her back. I told my grandma that my dad took his ex-wife back four times, two times he remarried, and guess what, she continued to cheat on him.

After the first divorce, I personally told my dad I did not want to see him hurt and to think about his decision. I was very young at the time, but still didn't think that was right for him to go back after what she did to him.

He stated he never raised one of his kids in the household and wanted to do this. At the end of the day, that was my dad's decision, and I had to accept that. I could not get upset or tell him not to take her back.

Imagine if he had left his wife for my wife; she would have remarried. She told me she was going to marry him. If this had happened, not one of my family members would give a damn about reaching out to her about returning to her husband, supporting her by calling and checking on her, or giving her money.

In addition, my family members would not even support me as we see now. My brother told my sister I wasn't answering the phone. He wanted to tell me not to go to court and settle with Leslie. I do not need anyone's advice or opinions, especially when they are not supportive and have never experienced what I am going through.

I could not even grieve for my dad, because as soon as I came back to Los Angeles, I had to grieve for my wife. The death of a marriage!

After realizing I am on my own in this world, cannot depend on anyone to support me, and constantly pray with and for me, I went into silence. God allowed my family, friends, and church members not to support me so he could show up and say, "I am the only support you need." Trust and believe in me, and I will guide you through the storm, and you will come out of the storm victorious. God said, "You are my chosen one, and I got you!" He said you remove yourself from social media at this time and that there is no need to respond to anyone. I also know no one owes me an explanation, and I do not owe anyone an explanation.

We recited and said, "To death do us part," yet this did not happen. In some countries, when a woman commits adultery, she would be subject to death. Imagine if this were the case in the United States, once a spouse commits adultery, you are subject to death. If we ever need population control, this would be the thing to do.

Also, people would think twice before scheming and having sex with other people while married. Also, one would think perhaps I should not get married if I will be a hoe and sleep with other people.

If that was not enough action for you, my son got into an accident and totally lost the family SUV. He was okay with no medical issues, which is a blessing. The devil was trying to attack my kids and me.

The evilness upon her was spreading. I prayed and prayed that all the evil of others would not harm my children or me. Since my separated wife did not add our son to the application as a household member, the insurance company did not pay and dropped me from the policy. This was a sad experience for my son and me. He was sad and cried about the situation.

I had to pay with savings to get the truck fixed. I had a difficult time finding insurance for myself. I found an insurance provider, but I had to pay more per month. I asked how much it cost to add my son so he can help me out by driving himself to work and school, and they told me $400 per month. I could not afford to pay that amount.

Due to having an accident and my son being young, the insurance was higher. He offered to pay for it, but I told him he would make that in two weeks, and this would not work. I could not add him to the insurance, and he could not drive any of the vehicles.

After posting, what one may call a cry for help, on my social media story, one of them stated, "When you go through hell, see who goes with you". Family members saw this, and then I had multiple texts and a phone call. This was about six months after the separation and four months after notifying my family. Thanks for reaching out after my cry for help, but that was too late for me. By then, I had already realized I was completely alone with my situation. I was literally going through hell, burning alone, with no one to save me.

It's crazy how the one who committed adultery and broke her family still receives all the love and support from everyone. I was left alone to die in pain and misery with no one caring about my kids and me. Not one person gave me a dime to support my kids or help pay for a meal, a bill, or anything. This is when I realized that when you're going through it, you really see who is there with you. I am thankful to God for revealing to me who people really are.

People say they care, but their actions do not show it. Although I will make a way and not depend on others, thank God, it is good when people show you they care, constantly praying with you, calling you, texting you constantly, and giving support; not asking or saying let me know if you need something several months later.

I will always be there for all five of my children and continue to pray for them and with them. I told them that as long as I am alive, I will be there to guide them, and I am here to talk with them. I will not just say it; I have conversations about things and ask questions because we as parents know we must engage our kids in conversation, or they will not share with us.

I always wondered why people commit suicide. Why would one want to kill oneself? I now see it.

When you've lost everything and feel unloved, unsupported, and alone, you fall into darkness and question why you're still here. Questioning if maybe I should have died and not my dad, since they cared and loved him and not me. You must be extremely strong in the Lord. You must pray consistently. You must control your mind and fight the demons that are attacking your soul.

The devil comes to kill, steal, and destroy. He sent people I loved to do this. You must read scripture and attend a supportive church to develop a strong mindset and know that this is a test from God and that it is only temporary. God tests us so often, and we often fail because we do not want to allow God to have his way. We want to have our way when we are going through things. Having faith in God may be difficult when you do not see a way out.

I have faith in God, and he told me everything will be alright in the end, my son. You are the chosen one, and if you stand strong with me, I will bless you exceedingly, abundantly, above all. You will have more than you asked for and even more than you imagine. God said I will provide your every need; all you have to do is trust in me and believe it. You must be patient; you must be ready for what I have in store for you, even though you do not yet see it.

I don't even know where I will be in 3-5 years. I used to know this, but now I do not even know. God said, you will be in a way better place and mindset by this time. God said I got you, chosen one, and I will not allow any weapon formed against you to prosper, just continue to share the Goodness of God.

I was already struggling with a mental disorder, for which I was receiving treatment. Even before the affair, I struggled daily with diabetes, high blood pressure, sleep apnea, and insomnia.

For years, I've been on anxiety meds, and it creeps up on me almost nightly. Now, to add to this, is double grief, losing my dad and my wife. Then adding depression, betrayal from family, friends, and church members is a lot for one person. Some days I feel like I am about to lose my mind, and then I break down and cry out to God to help me keep myself together. I pray and ask God to help me because I do not want to lose my mind, as I know he still has a purpose for me, and my kids need me, as I see no one else really cares about them.

My family members know exactly the health issues I battle with. Do you think they constantly check on me to see if I am taking my meds, how is my health, are you okay health-wise, did you see the doctor, how your body is feeling? Not one person reached out constantly to check on my mental and physical health. They just want to know if my divorce is final and what is going on so they can gossip about it. They can keep that fake love and what they call support.

I see exactly through them. They moved on with their lives while I went through hell, and they continued their daily routine. I will do the same, move on with my life, and continue my transformation and become God's chosen one.

Many families think that just because you are a man, you will be strong alone, get over it over time, and you must just be a man and suck it up. I must tell you, going through all that I've been through alone is the worst thing a man or anyone should have to go through alone.

She told someone, girl, he is going to come right back. He is a Christian, a good husband, a good father, and loves his family. He told me that he would never break up his family, and I have him on tape saying that to me. I will also share with him what he said he would never do. So, I will give him some time to heal, and watch him come back girl. I prayed for it as well. I went up for prayer and prayed to get my husband back in Jesus name. Amen!

When I found this out, I was like wow, she still has no accountability and does not accept anything that she has done to me. Now she is putting the divorce on me since I said I would never break up my family. Yet she was the one who left the marriage and said she was in love and was going to marry a married man. Since her plan did not work, she now wants to bring up the recording of me saying this in order for me to take her back. This is what you call narcissistic behavior. How would I even think about taking someone back like that? She never tried to apologize in person.

She just thought time would go by, that I would forget about it, and that we would be friends because we share kids. Just because you share kids with someone does not mean you have to be friends with them. I do not want to be friends with the enemy and hang out as if we are a family. As the Bible says in Proverbs 4:23, "Above all else, guard your heart, for everything you do flows from it."

God forbid I had done something drastic; then everyone would've said, "I wish he'd reached out or said something." I sent all the signs by informing them and posting stories on Instagram, but I noticed they saw every last one of them and did nothing. All that talk people give after something drastic happens just sounds nice; they rarely mean it. Family and Godparents did not constantly reach out to their Godchildren. One of the purposes of Godparents is to act as a support system for the child, offering guidance and encouragement throughout their life.

CHAPTER 10

FAITH OUTSIDE THE SANCTUARY

They say the church is a hospital for the broken, not a museum for the perfect. Yet when I arrived shattered, bleeding from betrayal, I did not find a place of healing. I found discomfort. I found the doors closing. I found people more concerned with image than truth.

Before everything fell apart, the church was my second home. I served faithfully, gave generously, and anchored my family there. We prayed together, fasted together, and raised our children within those walls. I believed we were more than a congregation; we were a spiritual family.

When my world collapsed after my wife's affair with a married fraternity brother, I thought church would be a safe place to fall apart. I was wrong. I expected compassion. I expected spiritual covering. I expected someone to see the weight I was carrying.

Instead, I noticed hesitation. Some people avoided me altogether, afraid they'd have to take a stand. Others offered shallow sympathy, quickly followed by, "You have to forgive, brother. You can't hold onto bitterness." Bitterness? Their words felt premature, almost instructional, as though my grief needed to follow a timetable that made everyone else more comfortable.

No one was asking her to repent. No one was confronting her. They were too busy protecting reputations. Too scared to confront sin when it wore a familiar face. I realized then that the rules were different when the offender had friends in high places.

Another told me I should "fight for my family," as if I hadn't already crawled through emotional fire trying to keep my home together. Their words weren't balm, they were salt in a raw wound. I started to feel like I was the problem. Not because of what I had done, but because I refused to stay silent. I refused to pretend everything was okay just to keep the peace in the pews.

Church folks I broke bread with started ghosting me. And just like that, the community I had poured my heart into evaporated. But the hardest part? Wrestling with God. I asked Him why.

I begged Him to make sense of the betrayal. I questioned everything I believed. Was any of it real? Did my prayers matter? Did God even see me?

It took time, months, maybe longer, but eventually, I found clarity. God didn't fail me; people did. The church had confused position with righteousness. They had confused unity with silence. They protected appearances at the cost of truth, and I was just collateral damage.

But God never abandoned me. I saw Him in quiet moments, late-night tears, the smile of my children, the strength I found when I thought I had none. He met me outside the sanctuary, in the stillness, when I had nothing left to offer but my brokenness. I no longer sit in those pews. But I haven't lost my faith.

In fact, my faith has become more real, stripped of performance, titles, and approval. I no longer serve to be seen. I no longer trust blindly. And I no longer confuse the voice of man with the voice of God. The church failed me. But grace didn't.

The Sunday right after my ex-wife was caught having an affair, I went to church with my kids. The pastor already knew what had happened because my ex called him on her flight back. I entered that sanctuary carrying more emotional weight than I had ever known. My mind was unraveling, and I needed prayer with an urgency I could barely contain.

Every week, there was an altar call. I really needed prayer as I was losing my mind. He did not call for an altar call. I was really hurt. I thought, wow, he knows my situation and maybe doesn't want me to share my prayer request aloud with the church. One of the church members was a famous actor. He and his wife are prayer warriors and cool with my wife and me. They both lead the church's marriage ministry.

The Sunday right after that happened, I went to church. I told him what happened, and he gave me his phone number. I texted him, and he never responded. I waited for a call or text back, but I never received one after several months had passed. I sent my kid's famous celebrity youth pastor a message through social media, and he never responded.

I was like, "Wow, so much for famous celebrity Christians when you need them." They post prayers on social media all the time, but when I need one, I get no response. I sent a message on Instagram to my kid's youth pastor's wife, and she responded with a brief reply, and that was it. I did not hear another word from her, or that she would notify her husband and have him pray and talk to the kids or me. Just silence from them.

I was crying out for help from the church folks, and they failed me, all of them. You really know who is for you when you go through hell. You find out exactly who needs to be in your life and who doesn't.

If I were going to do something really bad in retaliation, it would be those same family members, church members, and friends saying why would he do that. Why didn't he ask for help, etc.?

This is what I call fake love from fake Christians and friends. This is also why so many people, mainly men, do not share anything with anyone. We just suffer in silence because we don't receive support or feel supported by anyone around us.

Many people fall into depression or harm others after betrayal because no one offers true, nonjudgmental support. I have learned that no one truly gives a damn about you and your life, especially when you are going through hell.

It almost felt like those people enjoy seeing you struggle and go through hell since they are in a way better place than you. Also, others are so busy with their own lives that they do not have time to support you in yours. So, I get it, I will never count on family members, church members, and friends. I will only count on God; he will not let me down. I had to leave the church because I had already told my separated wife I would not worship with her.

After leaving the church, you would think any of the church members would reach out to my kids or me, but they did not. Weeks later, I received a general email sent to all married couples from the celebrity, who said he and his wife were hosting a marriage meeting for couples. I just unsubscribed from that email. How can you pray for couples in a marriage meeting when you ignored the man whose marriage was already destroyed?

That is crazy, ungodly work! You cannot pray for marriages with couples when it is working and when one falls apart, you ignore the cry for help. I just unsubscribed from that email. Not out of anger but out of acceptance. That chapter of my life had closed.

What surprised me most was what followed, a growing sense of spiritual independence. My relationship with God was no longer filtered through programs, personalities, or approval. It was personal, direct, and resilient.

Through this season, I also began to observe my former spouse differently. Distance has a way of sharpening vision. I saw how quickly someone can reshape a narrative to survive it, how easily conviction can be replaced by justification. Yet instead of fueling resentment, that awareness pushed me inward.

Who was I becoming through this? I realized I was no longer merely a man reacting to betrayal. I was becoming a man who understood his boundaries, his worth, and the sacred responsibility of guarding his heart. Faith, I learned, is not proven when life aligns with your expectations. Faith is revealed when everything familiar falls away and you still choose to trust God with what remains.

The church may not have held me the way I once imagined it would. But grace did. And in the quiet rebuilding of my life, I discovered something no silence could take from me. God was still present, still faithful, and still writing my story.

THE MIND'S COLLAPSE AND CURSE

WHEN THE MIND BREAKS

The house was silent, the kind of silence that presses against your ears, yet inside my mind there was nothing but noise. Thoughts collided, looped, and restarted like a song I could not turn off. I closed my eyes and tried to force sleep, but the moment darkness settled in, the images returned. Text messages I wished I had never seen. Words that did not belong to my marriage. A future that no longer existed. My chest tightened as I turned onto my side, then onto my back, then to the other side again. Nothing helped. Sleep, once a refuge, had become a place my body no longer trusted.

At first it had only been a few restless nights after discovering the affair. I told myself it was temporary, just shock, just grief. But the nights stretched longer. Two hours of sleep became one, then none at all. Soon

I began to dread nighttime because nighttime meant there were no distractions left.

No work, no conversations, no responsibilities loud enough to drown out the breaking inside me. Just me and the truth. Somewhere down the hallway, one of my children shifted in their sleep. The faint sound reminded me that morning would still come, lunches to pack, rides to coordinate, bills waiting to be paid. The world had not paused for my suffering, but my body had.

Exhaustion settled deep into my bones, yet my mind refused surrender. I got out of bed and walked into the kitchen, careful not to wake anyone. The tile was cold beneath my feet as I poured a glass of water and tried to steady my breathing. Inhale. Exhale. It did not help. Anxiety does not always arrive like a storm. Sometimes it slips in quietly, tightening its grip until you suddenly realize you cannot breathe the way you used to.

During the day it ambushed me without warning. Sitting in traffic, I would feel a wave rise from my stomach into my chest, heat, pressure, panic. My hands trembled on the steering wheel as I wondered what was happening to me. Even simple moments became unfamiliar. I would sit at the dinner table while my children talked and catch myself nodding without hearing a single word. Their laughter sounded distant, as though I were underwater. I was present in body but absent in spirit.

Nights were worse. Just as sleep approached, sleep apnea would jolt me awake, lungs grasping for air, heart pounding violently enough that I would sit upright convinced something inside me was failing. My own body had become unpredictable. I began forgetting things, misplacing items, losing track of conversations. Once known for my steadiness, I now felt like a man walking through fog. Beneath it all lived a quiet shame.

As a father, I believed I was supposed to be the strong one, the stable one, the protector. Instead, I was unraveling in the dark. I was already taking anxiety medications and sleep medication before my dad died and before the affair. My mind was already all over the place, mainly at night, and I just fought with myself.

I prayed often during those hours, not polished prayers, just raw whispers into the ceiling. "God, please let me sleep. God, quiet my mind. God, help me." Sometimes the only response was silence.

I wrestled with questions I was almost afraid to form. You revealed her betrayal so quickly, why not answer me now? Why leave me awake inside this suffering? Faith feels very different at three in the morning. It is less about theology and more about survival.

One sleep study test revealed that I stopped breathing seventeen times in a single night. I tried a CPAP machine, but the mask triggered even more anxiety, plastic pressed against my face, air forced into lungs that already felt overwhelmed. Instead of rest, I felt trapped, so I stopped using it.

I went to the doctor countless times again. I was issued multiple medications to help me sleep. Desperation makes you consider things you normally would not. I tried weed, wine, and hard liquor, and nothing seemed to work. I was at war with myself at night, and I was losing the fight. I felt ashamed. Ashamed of not being strong enough. Ashamed of breaking down. As a man, as a father, as someone people once looked to for stability, it was humiliating to admit I was unravelling. But I was.

There were nights I woke and reached for medication, only to freeze halfway through the motion, unable to remember what I had already taken. A terrifying thought followed, what if I take the wrong one? Some prescriptions warned clearly not to combine them with alcohol because of the high risk of death. The word lingered longer than it should have. One night, glass in hand, I stared at the bottle and realized how thin the line between relief and danger had become. I set it down, not because I was not tired, but because my children still needed their father.

That realization anchored me more than anything else. Long before the affair, sleep had been a struggle. Since high school I had leaned on sleep aids, chasing rest that never fully came. Through college and into adulthood, the pattern continued. But betrayal magnified everything.

Grief layered upon exhaustion. Anxiety layered upon heartbreak. Soon, I made a decision that frightened me but also brought clarity. I resigned from multiple jobs and kept only one. Financially, it made no sense, but my mind was breaking, and no paycheck was worth losing myself.

I knew this affair caused my mental state and health to decline. I was about to lose my mind trying to raise five kids, with not one family member reaching out to lend a helping hand. Yet, my family, my wife's side of the family, church members, and friends all gave her money to support her, knowing what she did.

Not one person offered me a dime! My friend said to me, it's very sad that no one is supporting you when she was the one who did all the damage. He said that if you had plotted to leave her for a married woman she knew well, they would have talked about you like a dog and never supported you. I said exactly, you are right. People think that just because you are a man, you are going to be okay and strong.

For the first time, survival became more important than productivity. There were moments I looked around and felt profoundly alone, raising five children while my internal world trembled. It seemed others assumed I would simply endure because I was a man. Strength is often expected and rarely supported. Yet even in that loneliness, I began noticing something subtle. I was still here. Still waking up. Still praying. Still choosing not to give up. And that mattered.

Mental illness does not announce itself with visible scars. It lives quietly in sleepless nights, racing thoughts, and shallow breaths. But I have learned that struggling does not make you weak; it makes you human. Healing is not linear. Some nights are still long, and some mornings I wake more tired than when I lay down. Anxiety may still live with me. Sleep may still be a struggle. But I've stopped pretending that I'm okay when I'm not.

Yet somewhere along the way, my perspective shifted. Instead of asking when this would end, I started asking what it was teaching me. It was teaching me humility, the courage to admit I needed help. It was teaching me compassion, because you never know what silent battles others are fighting. Most of all, it was teaching me endurance.

Some victories are quiet. Sometimes courage is simply staying. Sometimes surviving is the miracle. And when dawn finally breaks after another sleepless night, I remind myself of one simple truth, I made it through the dark again. For now, that is enough.

CHAPTER 12

THE BREAKING POINT

There was a moment, one I'm not proud of, when I no longer recognized the man staring back at me in the mirror. It was early morning, the kind of quiet that settles over a house before the sun rises. The children were still asleep, their doors closed, their breathing steady and unaware of the tension that had taken residence in our home. I stood at the kitchen counter holding a mug of coffee that had long since gone cold, watching Leslie move through the hallway without looking at me. We barely spoke.

That was when the weight of what I had done settled in. I had taken her back. Not because forgiveness had come. Not because trust had been rebuilt. I took her back because the alternative felt too heavy to carry. The silence in the house after she left had been unbearable, echoing through every room.

The kids had started asking questions I could not answer. Their eyes searched my face for reassurance I did not possess. And somewhere beneath the anger and humiliation, a small, stubborn part of me, God help me, still wanted to believe she could become the woman I married again.

When we did, her words were flat, like they'd been edited for safety. I watched her closely, waiting for signs of remorse, guilt, or, worse, indifference. And that's what I saw, indifference. Like she'd detached from it all, from me. She seemed more bothered by the discomfort of confrontation than the damage of betrayal.

Something in me snapped. I don't know how to explain it, except to say I felt like I was drowning in rage. The anger did not arrive as shouting or slammed doors. It was quieter than that. More controlled. More dangerous. It lived beneath my skin, steady and simmering.

I would sit across from her at the dinner table, listening to the ordinary sounds of forks against plates, and feel a wave rise in my chest so strong I had to grip the edge of the chair to ground myself. I was not just hurting. I was changing. One morning, after another sleepless night, I found myself standing in our bathroom.

The overhead light was harsh, exposing the exhaustion carved into my face. My eyes were bloodshot. My jaw was tight. I barely looked human to myself. And then the thoughts came, dark, intrusive, an uninvited.

I imagined what it would feel like to take control of the narrative the way control had been stolen from me. I imagined restraining her emotionally, surrounding her with the same suffocating silence I had endured. I wanted her to feel trapped inside the consequences she seemed able to walk past. For a fleeting moment, an image crossed my mind, my hands around her throat, not to end her life, but to force the truth out of her.

To shake loose the lies. To make her understand the magnitude of the pain she had delivered so casually. In that same instant, another image followed, panic and regret. Horror at what I was capable of imagining. My fists tightened at my sides as I stared into the mirror.

No violence had occurred. No words had been spoken. No hands had moved. But inside my mind, I had crossed a line. And it terrified me. Because that's what betrayal does.

It doesn't just break your heart; it tries to remake you into someone hardened, suspicious, and unfamiliar. Someone driven less by love and more by injury. Standing there, chest rising and falling rapidly, I realized I was not just fighting for my marriage anymore. I was fighting for my identity. I refused to become a man ruled by rage.

That morning, before I could talk myself out of it, I picked up the phone and called a therapist. I told them everything. Not just about her, about me. The thoughts, the rage, and the dreams. The fear that I was becoming something twisted.

That phone call marked the beginning of real healing. Not the polished healing people talk about in public. Not the performative strength we show the world. This was raw, uncomfortable, stripped of pride. The kind of healing that meets you on the floor when you finally admit you cannot carry the weight alone.

There were days I cried in my car before walking into the house, wiping my face so my children would not see. Nights when I buried my face in a pillow just to muffle the sound of grief leaving my body. Journal pages filled with words I never imagined writing, confessions I could barely bring myself to reread. It was ugly work. But it was honest.

Looking back now, I can see that this was my lowest point, yet strangely, it was also my first truly authentic one. Pain has a way of stripping away illusion until all that remains is truth. And the truth was this; I was deeply wounded, but I was not beyond repair. If you have ever been betrayed and caught yourself thinking thoughts you are ashamed to admit, hear me clearly, those thoughts do not make you evil.

They make you human. Wounded people sometimes wander into dark emotional territory. The danger is not in the thought itself; the danger is choosing to live there. I knew I could not allow my woundedness to define me. I had not survived all of this just to transform into another source of harm.

So, I made a decision. I chose truth over silence.

Help over pride.

Healing over denial. And day by day, piece by piece, I began the brutal, sacred work of putting myself back together.

CHAPTER 13

THE DREAM THAT WOKE ME UP SCREAMING

T he night started with me glancing at the clock beside my bed. 2:17 a.m. The house was silent except for the low hum of the fan and the occasional creak of settling wood. I had fallen asleep out of pure exhaustion, not peace. Sleep had become something my body forced on me when it could no longer stay awake. And then the dream came.

In it, I had been driving for six hours. The road stretched endlessly ahead, illuminated only by my headlights cutting through the darkness. Music blasted through the speakers, loud enough to drown out thought, yet every lyric seemed to echo my pain. My hands gripped the steering wheel tighter than necessary. I had been driving for hours, though I could not remember where I started or where I was going. I wasn't headed to a destination. I was chasing my pain into darkness.

Eventually, I turned onto a quiet residential street and stopped across from a house I instantly recognized. James' house, the man who ruined my family, my fraternity brother. The one who looked me in the eye while sleeping with Leslie. In the dream, information had come easily, addresses, routines, where he parked his car. Rage had made me methodical.

The neighborhood lights flickered off one by one as midnight deepened. I stepped out of the car and moved through the darkness like someone who no longer feared consequences. My fingers trembled, not from the cold, but from something volcanic inside me. I crouched beside his vehicle and planted an explosive beneath it. Then I drove away.

When morning came, I returned and parked across the street, engine off, like a predator waiting for its justice. My chest rose and fell slowly, as if justice were about to unfold. The front door opened. James came out of the house, but he wasn't alone. He had his son with him. My stomach dropped.

The boy's voice was light, innocent, untouched by the destruction I had imagined. James opened the car door and motioned for him to get in. Then he paused. "Wait," he said casually. "I forgot something." He turned back toward the house. The boy called after him, "Dad! Can I start the car so I can listen to music?"

"No," James replied without looking back. "I forgot something." The innocence in that exchange shattered whatever rage had been holding me upright. That child had nothing to do with my pain. Nothing to do with betrayal. And yet, in the dream, I had placed him in harm's way. Panic seized me.

Before I could think, I jumped out of my car and hurried toward the vehicle, desperate to stop what I had set in motion. My legs moved faster than my thoughts. I crouched near the tires, desperate to flatten them, to stop this. To somehow save a life I never intended to threaten. But before I could act, the door swung open.

He stepped out, holding whatever he'd gone back for. My eyes met his for a split second, long enough for my blood to freeze. I turned, walked slowly back to my car, pretending I was nobody. Just a stranger on a quiet street. He opened the car door, climbed in, and started the engine.

The explosion was instant. The fire, the sound, the shockwave, it swallowed everything. And both of them, he and his son, were gone. Fire erupted. The sound ripped through the air. The shockwave hit my chest like a physical blow. And both of them were gone.

I woke up screaming. Heart racing so hard it felt like it would break my ribs. Sweat soaked my sheets. My lungs couldn't get air. For several seconds, I did not know where I was. Reality and nightmare blurred together until I forced myself to sit upright. "It was just a dream," I whispered over and over, gripping the mattress.

But the guilt lingered. Because even though I would never commit such an act, my mind had gone there. Pain had dragged me to an edge I didn't know existed. Sleep offered no refuge after that.

Another night, another dream. This time, I was standing outside a crowded club, watching James through the window. Music pulsed through the walls. Laughter spilled into the street. In the dream, everything felt deliberate, calculated.

I sent a woman in with money to buy a drink for the guy standing on the right, next to the two other guys in white shirts who look like a snowman. I gave her a little more money to flirt with him and leave with him. He is a weak man, so I knew that would work. I watched as she guided him toward her car. His friends laughed, shouting their approval as he stumbled along beside her.

By the time they reached the vehicle, he was barely steady. I followed them down a dark road until the car slowed. Together, we struggled to get his fat ass in. Every motion felt heavy, surreal, like I was watching someone else live inside my skin. The girl flagged down a car in effort to help.

Suddenly, headlights approached. A police cruiser. I was like fuck, I cannot be seen here with a cop. The cop stopped by and asked if everything was okay. She said yes, her friend had too much to drink and was throwing up.

He asked why did you stop us, and she said because I thought you were the friend we lost after leaving dinner, and they were following us. The cops then proceeded to leave. I looked around, saying man that was a close one.

We both laughed with scared anxiety. I told her please pay attention to who you stop next time.

Eventually, with the help of a stranger, we moved him into my car. I then drove six hours to bring him to an abandoned place I had already prepared for. This place had all the necessary tools for preparing for surgery. What I did not tell you is that I am a doctor, but I did not finish medical school. I was able to get all the medical supplies I needed to prepare for the big day, the surgery.

At this place, I had a big dolly to use to try to carry him. However, I told myself this is too nice of me. After opening the car door, I let him fall to the ground. When he woke, confusion flooded his face. "What are you doing?" he demanded.

I said get your fat, ugly ass up and go in this building if you want to stay alive. He then proceeded to the building. I told him to sit on the bed, he said no I am not doing shit until you tell me what is going on. I showed him a picture of his son.

"If you want to see him again," I said, "you'll do exactly what I tell you." Even in the dream, the words felt foreign in my mouth. He sat on the bed, and then I gave him a shot that knocked him out. He fell back and then I untied him and then handcuffed him to the bed. I proceeded to give him anesthesia as I was preparing for surgery.

I removed both of his middle fingers as he did not give two fucks about my life and my kids' lives. I also removed his ring finger since he did not care about his marriage. The abandoned building was an hour from my house.

I went back home, got my kids ready for school. When Leslie was coming to pick up our daughter to go to daycare, I asked her to come in and please finish get her ready for school while I used the restroom.

She proceeded to come in, and then I shot her with a needle that knocked her out. She then fell out, and I held her to lie on the sofa. I had already brought my daughter to daycare. I put my wife in the car; she is smaller than her heavy, future husband, so it was easy for me. I drove to the abandoned building where she can be with her future husband.

I sat her in the bed and began performing surgery on her. Guess what I removed from her body? You guessed it! I removed both of her middle fingers as she did not give two fucks either. I also removed her ring finger for the same reason.

I was kind enough to create a recovery room for them, filled with pictures of his kids and my kids. I put pictures of them together. I even put pictures of his kids, my kids, and the two of them together. He was on social media posting family pictures along with his wife, so those pictures were so easy to get and put together. With the help of AI, they put all the kids together as if it were a single picture.

When I moved them to the recovery room, they both woke up to look at the slide show I had prepared. Both have masking tape on their mouth, handcuffs to the bed, and a cask on each hand. They were trying to move and move their mouths in panic as they looked at the slideshow and at each other. As they woke up to understand what may be happening, I decided to go fix myself some alcohol. I unwrapped the hand bandages on both.

They both noticed their middle and ring fingers were gone. I then showed them, is this what you are looking for laughing with rage in my eyes.

I then woke up with my heart racing, thinking the dream was real. I had to get out of bed to breathe and calm down, and I drank lots of water. I had to pray and ask God to take these dreams away. But the nights continued. Sometimes the setting changed.

The Dreams I Couldn't Control

There were nights when sleep wasn't peace; it was war. In my dreams, I wasn't myself. I was a version of me stripped of reason, broken by betrayal, burning with a rage so deep I didn't recognize my own face. I saw her, my wife, laughing with him. The man I once called a fraternity brother.

And I'd feel it rise in me, something animal, something ancient. I'd shout, curse, grab, and lash out. I didn't care about the consequences in those dreams. I just wanted them to feel a fraction of what I felt. In one dream, I stood over them, fists clenched, heart racing, ready to destroy what they had destroyed in me.

And then I'd wake up sweating, shaking, heart pounding, tears already falling. I hated those dreams. I never wanted to hurt anyone, not in real life. But my subconscious had no filter. My pain had nowhere else to go.

In Depth: Dreams in the Dark

There's a place my mind would go when I was asleep, far from reason, far from grace. A place where pain spoke louder than my conscience. I didn't ask to go there. I didn't want to. But night after night, my dreams took me to the edge of something I was terrified to face.

They weren't just nightmares. They were explosions of emotion: rage, betrayal, grief, humiliation all tangled together in vivid, and terrifying detail.

The Hotel Room: It always started the same. I was outside a hotel room. I knew they were inside, my wife and him, her secret lover, the man I once called "fraternity brother." I could hear them laughing. The sound boiled my blood.

I kicked the door open. She screamed. He stood up like he could challenge me. I rushed him. My fists found his face, again and again, until I couldn't recognize it anymore. I turned to her, and she backed into a corner.

"Why?" I shouted. "After all I gave you… why?" And then I'd wake up, fists clenched, soaked in sweat. Gasping. Hating the man I became in that dream, but even more, hating the reason he existed.

The Church: It was a Sunday morning. We were sitting in church as if nothing had happened. The congregation was singing, hands lifted high. My wife was beside me, hands raised too, like she was pure, untouched, holy. He walked in, her future husband in disguise, my fraternity brother.

The congregation clapped as if he were a returning hero. And I stood there screaming, "Do you not see what they did?!" No one heard me.

I pulled out a gun in the dream, not to shoot, but to force them to see. I demanded truth, justice, and accountability.

But all they did was keep singing. My wife looked at me, calm and cruel, and said, "You're the only one who's broken." I woke up sobbing. Because even in my dream, the world refused to hold them accountable.

The Cliff: We were on a road trip, she and the kids. Like old times. But the road twisted into a mountain cliff. She whispered to him while I drove. I knew. I always knew.

At the top, I stopped the car. Asked her to step out. She did, without fear. The wind was howling. She said something that still echoes in my bones, "You weren't enough for me. He was."

I lunged. In the dream, I pushed her. I watched her fall. Then I woke up screaming, horrified, and shaking. Not because she died in the dream, but because I let her.

The Fire: I was back in our home. The kids were away. She and he were in our bedroom, our sacred space. The rage was nuclear. I didn't touch them.

I lit a match instead. Set the bed on fire. Stood in the hallway while the flames rose. They screamed from inside. I just stood there.

When my mind went to sleep, it let the storm out. A beast was being released. The dreams left me feeling empty for days. Because I realized something, I didn't want revenge. I wanted release. I wanted it all to burn so I wouldn't have to feel anything anymore. I never told anyone about these dreams.

Not at first. I feared what they said about me. A husband, a father, and a man of faith. Someone who had always believed in justice, not vengeance. But I am human. I had been deeply wronged, and the wound bled into everything, even my rest. I learned that dreams are not sins. They are screams from a soul in agony. They are grief unspoken. Pain unhealed and anger suppressed.

I never laid a hand on her. I never confronted him with violence. But in my dreams, I did things I could never do in life. And those dreams terrified me; not just for what they showed, but for what they revealed. I was deeply hurt, broken, and on the verge of losing not just her, but myself.

It took time, therapy, prayer, and brutal honesty to face those dreams. To admit them. To write them. And to forgive myself for having them. If you are reading this and you have had thoughts you are ashamed of, thoughts that feel dark, twisted, or out of character, I need you to hear that you are not alone.

What I came to understand is that those dreams didn't make me a monster. They made me a man in grief. A man whose love had been violated. A man whose mind was trying to survive a heartbreak, it didn't know how to heal. And I got help. I talked, I prayed, and I wept.

I confessed those dreams to God. I chose not to act in rage. I chose to feel it, face it, and release it. Again, and again. That choice didn't come easy. But it saved me.

Pain has its own language. And sometimes, it speaks in fire and fists when what it really wants is to be held. I'm not proud of those dreams. But I'm proud I survived them.

CHAPTER 14

THE CURSE THAT WAS NEVER BROKEN

I used to believe we were free. By loving my wife, being present for my kids, and faithfully showing up for my church and family, I was breaking generational cycles. But betrayal has a way of peeling back everything you thought was healed. Suddenly, I wasn't just dealing with her choices. I was staring at patterns, ugly and hidden, woven through the bloodline I came from, patterns of silence.

Shame, secrets, abandonment, and violence. Emotional neglect passed off as "strength." It hit me like a brick. This wasn't just about her affair. This was about all the men before me. All the women before her.

The family I came from. We had fathers who weren't there emotionally. Present, maybe, but unavailable. Apologies were rare. Vulnerability? Never.

My mother carried it all. And she passed down the lessons, survive, don't trust, and hide your pain.

I had uncles who disappeared. Cousins raised in chaos. Molestation swept under the rug. Family members who cheated, lied, walked out, and covered it all with religion or silence. Verbal and physical abuse becomes the norm. We don't talk about what hurts us. We keep moving like ghosts.

It's no wonder I didn't see the red flags early on. I was trained not to. The woman I married had her own history, wounds I didn't fully understand. I can look back now and see it; the way she needed validation, feared confrontation, craved praise, but resisted responsibility. She carried generational pain, too. But instead of facing it with me, she passed it on. She let the curse live through her betrayal.

The Church That Missed It

Even the church, the place that should have broken these chains, often just dressed them up in scripture. We preach about blessings, but we whisper about abuse. We praise God loudly but ignore mental illness quietly. We call women "virtuous" but ignore their trauma. We call men "head of household" but ignore their burdens. So, the curses continue.

What Is a Generational Curse?

It's not just superstition or folklore. Its trauma left untreated. Its bitterness passed down. It's a family pattern of dysfunction that nobody wants to name.

- A grandfather cheats, a father cheats, a son cheats, and vice versa.
- A mother enables, a daughter denies, a granddaughter repeats.
- Emotional unavailability becomes the norm.
- Silence becomes survival.
- Anger becomes an inheritance.

And if no one confronts it, then it just keeps going.

Breaking the Curse

After the affair, I was standing at a crossroads. Not just for myself, but for my kids. For my sons and daughters. I couldn't let this be their inheritance.

So, I started saying the things no one ever said to me:

- "I'm hurting."
- "I don't know how to fix this, but I won't pretend I'm okay."
- "I forgive, but I also set boundaries."
- "We will talk about hard things."
- "Therapy is not weakness."
- "God is not a bandage for denial."

Choosing a New Legacy

Breaking a curse doesn't happen in one day. It happens every day you choose to feel instead of being numb. Every day, you choose truth over image. Every time you say, "This ends with me."

It's hard. It's lonely sometimes. But I'd rather be the one who breaks the pattern than the one who repeats it. Because curses might run in bloodlines, but so can healing.

Your children are watching, learning, and inheriting not only your wounds, but your healing. They don't say much. But they watch everything. My kids have seen more than I ever wanted them to.

They saw the smiles in family photos and the tension in our silence. They heard "I love you" at bedtime and muffled arguments behind closed doors.

They've watched me hold it together, and they've watched me fall apart. And the most haunting part of all? They're learning how to be people. From me.

I Don't Want to Pass This Down

The anger, the silence, the emotional shutdowns, the need to "stay strong" even when everything inside is breaking. That's what was passed to me. That's what I inherited. But it's not what I want to give to them.

What I Started Doing

I started doing things that felt awkward at first:

- Saying "I'm sorry" when I lose my temper.
- Letting them see me cry, then explaining why.
- Talking about feelings. Not lectures, not sermons, just honest conversations.
- Saying "It's okay to be angry, but you have to know what to do with it."
- Praying out loud with them, not to perform, but to model surrender.
- Telling the truth about mistakes, including mine.

I started parenting not from perfection, but from presence. Because healing doesn't mean never hurting. It means learning how to hurt honestly, and love through it.

Teaching My Sons

I told them being a man is not about control. It's about stewardship of your emotions, your words, and your actions. It's okay to feel. It's not okay to destroy. Love means responsibility and accountability.

I remind them that anger is natural, but revenge is not strength. And that loving a woman doesn't mean losing yourself. I show them that when trust is broken, you don't have to become a breaker too.

Teaching My Daughters

I told them you are not responsible for a man's choices. You are not defined by anyone's love or betrayal. And you are never too much or too little to be cherished just as you are.

I make sure they know how to speak up. How to say no. How to ask for help. How to value themselves without needing someone else's validation. And I pray that when they grow, they'll recognize love that looks like truth, not control.

I Still Fail

Some days I say too little. Some nights I retreat. Sometimes they ask hard questions, and I don't have answers. But they know I'm trying. They know I'm here. And I hope, one day, they'll say, "My father was broken, but he didn't break us."

Generational curses are real, and this has gone on too long within my family and many families. We expect others to just pray to God and ask him to find it in our hearts to forgive and just move on. This is because this is what they did. One or both spouses cheated on each other, and they just moved on. One spouse cheat, then the other one cheats, then they just move on because they're even.

They both stay in the marriage because of the kids. In many marriages, we have people who committed adultery and have kids outside the marriage, and they stayed.

When I was in first grade, my mom and I caught my dad in bed with another woman. I called him a fucka bitch. At that time, my mother left my dad.

However, she already knew he was cheating, as my half-brother is nine days older than I am. At the time, some of my dad's family supported my dad's mistress rather than my mom, his wife. My mother also experienced betrayal from a spouse, family members, church members, and friends. For too long, women and men stay in toxic marriages only because of the kids. At the end of the day, who really hurts are the kids.

I acted out at the young age of four. I demonstrated the violence and behavior I saw. I bullied kids at school. I was very active and bad, as they called it. I was put on multiple medications at the age of 8 because of my attention and behavior, which led to a mental disorder.

I had multiple learning disabilities and had a resource teacher to help me read, speak, and comprehend. My mom made sure I had the resources needed to succeed, and I really thank her for that and for not giving up on me as a struggling kid with mental issues. She did an amazing job and never gave up on me growing up. I say this to inform all parents that if your marriage or relationship is toxic and kids are involved. Seek spiritual guidance from God; he is the only one who can guide you.

Pray daily, fast, read your bible, and ask God to order your steps. We must be careful letting family and friends into our marriage, especially if they're not strong in the Lord, as their advice may not fit our situation. You can also seek spiritual counseling and a family therapist. Still, it's tricky, as these individuals must truly have your best interests at heart and understand what God is revealing to you. No one should tell you what to do in your marriage, whether to divorce or not.

This decision is up to you. Pray to God to help you with your life-changing decision. I prayed to God constantly and fasted on some days. I needed God to speak to me and guide me.

I entered a period of relative silence, as I did not want to speak with any of my family members. After losing trust in family members and feeling unsupported, I decided not to share any of my personal business with them.

I saw where it led me. This led to a decline in my mental health. I was already dealing with multiple mental issues before the divorce. I did not want to hear all these opinions and horrible advice from people. Past experiences, yours or others, don't give anyone the right to tell you whether to stay in your marriage or what to do. If someone is seeking advice or an opinion, then family members or friends need to first pray to God alone to help guide them on what Godly advice to share with their hurt friend.

Then you should pray together with that person. Also, you need to understand that most of the time, that person just needs a non-judgmental person to talk to and for you to just listen. Often, individuals know what they need to do when they keep God first; they just need a listening ear to guide them as they work through the issues in their minds. Many generations have dealt with family trauma and drama with individuals, and they would stop talking to family members for a while. Over time, we will all just forget what happened and get back to how we used to be.

Many think that, over time, the pain, suffering, betrayal, and disrespect just fade away, and we should just forget because we are family. I am breaking the curse of allowing people to disrespect, not show support, and betray me by moving in silence and loving from a distance. I don't need apologies or opinions; I'm just moving on, the same way everyone did while I was suffering inside. And if anyone was sorry or needed to share something, they would have communicated that with me.

Just a text and an email can go a long way if you are truly sorry. However, you have family members who do not even think they did anything wrong. They have no clue about what I know certain individuals were saying and doing behind my back. God revealed to me who my family, friends, and church members really are, and I am thankful for that. I must distance myself from people who are not for me. Grieving the living is very difficult, but needed to protect your peace.

This is difficult, but my peace is worth it. I do not owe anyone an explanation. I am moving on, I choose peace. My peace is my distance and love from afar. I feel so much better now, not having to explain my situation to others who do not care or have my best interest in mind, with me having five kids. I feel at peace not sharing my personal business with others, who tend to be negative when I share things.

Many of these individuals would not share anything about their personal lives but wanted to know every move you made. Pretty interesting how these people are, and they are your family and friends. I feel at peace not hearing gossip about my siblings, uncles, aunts, cousins, family members, and friends. I feel at peace not hearing negativity from individuals. I feel at peace, minding my own business and not caring about others.

After all the horrible things my ex-wife did to the kids and me, you have my family and friends asking about reconciliation, and just find it in your heart to forgive. They just want me to forgive and forget the plotting and horrible things she did. No one going through this would ever forget what someone has done to them.

And just because the man she was supposed to marry, after eventually settling with me, did not leave his wife for her, I'm just supposed to just forgive and take her back. This is straight bullshit.

Also, this is because they have done this for generations. I will break that generational curse in the mighty name of Jesus. I told my friend, now what if I had stayed just for the kids, since that's what family and friends' advice was, and I just snapped one night and strangled her. What would my family and friends say then? Probably feel bad for telling me to stay with an ungrateful wife.

When someone shows you who they are, believe them the first time. They are only sorry because they got caught. The plotting, scheming, and planning against you; there is no coming back to that. No weapon formed against me shall prosper, says the Lord. She formed the weapon; however, it did not prosper.

She had prayers as well. She prayed for her new husband, another woman's husband, you have to be some type of stupid to pray for another woman's husband. That is beyond evil. She even once told me, "How you get them is also how you lose them". So eventually, what she did would also eventually happen to her.

My friend shared that he was listening to an old-school song, and the lady said, "God's not going to give you someone else's husband." He said, "I thought about your wife." That was funny.

God works in mysterious ways. I serve an awesome God. We have to be done with people. It is okay to love your family from a distance. I will never allow one person to ever betray me.

You only get one time to betray me. Do not let the same snake bite you twice. So much betrayal happened in the bible, so who am I to think it would never happen to me? Joseph was betrayed by his brothers, and God made the same brothers need Joseph for food. Do not worry about those people who treated you badly.

The users, manipulators, self-centered, and narcissistic people will get the karma that they deserve. God will fight my battles for me. Peace be to them after the consequences that God sees fit for them. May God have mercy on their souls. You must remove yourself from these types of people, regardless of who they are.

The majority of the time, it is your family and friends. It hurts differently when you know you did nothing but have a helpful heart, and no one supports you. When a person is going through hell, and you know it, family, friends, and church members should be there constantly for you.

CHAPTER 15

THE RETRAINING ORDER

I t was late afternoon when I heard my youngest daughter's laughter coming from the living room, that sweet, careless sound that calmed me. I had been working in the house all day, trying to hold life together with one hand while typing and answering calls with the other. We were separated, and Leslie had already taken my daughter away once, so every moment I had with her felt fragile, like something that could be snatched back without warning.

I kept telling myself to stay steady, to stay calm, because the kids were watching everything even when they didn't speak. When my daughter came back the following week, I tried to make the night normal. I cooked dinner, cleaned up, and kept the routine moving like I always did.

Bath time was the one part of the day that slowed everything down. The house was quieter upstairs, the warm water fogged the mirror, and my daughter splashed like nothing in the world could touch her.

I washed her hair, lifted her arm to rinse the soap, and that's when I saw it. Five clear finger marks on her left side, dark enough to stop my breath. For a second, I just stared, trying to make sense of what I was looking at. My stomach turned. My throat tightened. I ran my hand gently near the marks, careful not to press them, and asked her, "Baby, does that hurt?"

She looked at me with her wide eyes and said, "Yes." Something in me snapped. Not in a dramatic way, not with yelling or throwing things, but with that cold, instant switch that happens when your body decides it has to protect what it loves. I grabbed my phone, took a picture, and texted Leslie immediately. My fingers moved fast, angry and shaking.

I sent the photo and wrote, "What happened to her? Why does she have handprints on her side?" I expected panic, concern, some explanation, anything that sounded like a mother taking it seriously. Instead, she replied like I was bothering her over nothing.

"That's nothing." Just that. No questions. No concern. No urgency. "That's nothing." I stared at the message as if I didn't understand English anymore. I texted again, sharper this time. "That is not nothing. Those are five finger marks. She says it hurts. What did you do?" My anger wasn't just about the bruises.

It was about the way she brushed it off, the way she kept minimizing everything, the way she acted like I was irrational for noticing what was happening to our child. I kept thinking, if a daycare worker saw those marks, they would report it. If a teacher saw those marks, they would report it. But the one person who was supposed to care most was telling me it was nothing.

That night, while the kids were settling into bed, I heard pounding at the front door. Not a knock. A bang. Over and over, loud enough to shake the frame and make the house feel unsafe. I looked through the window and saw Leslie on the porch, face tight, posture aggressive, hitting the door like she was trying to break it down. My daughter, already sensitive from the chaos of the separation, started crying immediately.

Her crying turned into screaming when the banging didn't stop. It wasn't just noise anymore. It was fear. The kind of fear that makes a child's whole-body shake. I opened the door only enough to speak through the gap.

"You can't come in. The kids are going to bed. Please leave," I said, trying to keep my voice steady. She leaned in, eyes hard, and said, "Half this house is mine," like she was daring me to challenge her. I could see neighbors stepping outside, looking toward our porch, drawn by the sound and the tension.

I felt humiliated, but more than that, I felt protective. The kids didn't deserve this. They didn't deserve to hear their mother pounding on the door like a stranger, turning our home into a scene. "Please stop," I told her. "You're scaring them." She kept banging.

My daughter's screams got louder. I took Ilana upstairs and had Will stay with her, then I came back down and tried again. "Leave. Now. If you don't, I'm going to have to report this. And I'm taking our daughter to the doctor because of those marks."

That's when she screamed, almost smiling when she said it, "That's why I called the cops." The words landed like ice water. A few minutes later, the police arrived. The porch lights lit up their uniforms, and our driveway filled with that unmistakable sense of public judgment. I stepped outside, hands open, speaking carefully.

Leslie stayed loud until the officer warned her about disturbing the peace. Only then did her volume drop. I explained everything to them about our separation, the marks on our daughter, the banging at the door, the fear in the house. The officers asked to take photographs of the bruises and asked if they could question my daughter. I agreed, and my chest tightened as they spoke to her gently, trying to find the truth through a three-year-old's words.

When they asked where it happened, she answered, simple and clear, "At my mommy house." The officer looked at me and nodded like he already knew what that meant. "We have to report this," he said. "You need to have her examined." They told Leslie to leave the property and not disturb the peace, and she dropped into tears outside like a switch flipped, collapsing to the ground and crying loud enough for the neighbors to hear. But the officers didn't move toward her like she expected.

They didn't rush to comfort her. They stayed focused, calm, professional, and that alone felt like a small mercy. The next day, I went to the courthouse to file the restraining order paperwork, following the officers' advice. I didn't realize it would take all day. I had no family nearby.

No one to watch my daughter. So, I pushed her stroller through long lines, through metal detectors, through the slow shuffle of bureaucracy while she asked for snacks and cartoons and I tried to keep my face neutral. The court closed for lunch, and they told us to come back later. I walked back out into the sun, exhausted, feeling like the system expected me to function like I wasn't drowning.

By the time I finished the paperwork, it was late afternoon. I walked out of the courthouse with my daughter in her stroller, thinking we were finally headed home. That's when I saw Leslie. She was coming toward us fast, eyes locked, moving with the kind of energy that makes your body brace before your mind catches up. I barely had time to react before she reached for the stroller, grabbing it like she was snatching property, not approaching a child.

My daughter started crying instantly, startled by the aggression and the suddenness. "What are you doing?" I said. "You're scaring her." Leslie snapped back, "That's my daughter," and tried to pull the stroller away. I tightened my grip, not to fight her, but to keep the stroller stable. Leslie yanked harder.

The wheels jerked sideways. My daughter screamed. I pleaded, "Stop. Please leave us alone." But she pulled again, and the stroller tipped, just enough to make my heart stop.

Instinct took over. I grabbed the handle with both hands and forced it upright so my daughter wouldn't slam face-first into concrete.

If I hadn't strapped her in properly, she would've been thrown. If I had let go, she would've been hurt. That thought hit me like nausea. Then Leslie began screaming at the top of her lungs. "Help! Somebody help me! He's hurting me!"

Her voice echoed off the courthouse walls, loud enough to turn heads, loud enough to rewrite the scene for anyone who didn't see the beginning. And I realized, with a cold clarity, what she was doing. She was building a story in real time. She was trying to turn me into the villain in front of witnesses. So, I screamed too, because I didn't know what else to do.

"Help! She's attacking our daughter and me!" My daughter shook in the stroller, crying so hard she couldn't catch her breath. Leslie kept grabbing, yanking, falling, flailing, and then stumbling backward into bushes, bruising herself in the chaos she created. At that time, I was running with the stroller to reach the truck and get my daughter to safety.

After she recovered from her fall, she tried a third time to attach us, and by that time, the court Sheriff was coming. She lied to the Sheriff about what happened and said I attacked her. She was crying, falling on the ground. She stated that I bruised her and showed them all the bruises she had from flying back in the bushes after she attacked us. In a trembling voice, I told the Sheriff I am leaving the courthouse, pushing my baby in a stroller, how in the world can I attack somebody?

That makes no sense. There was an outside officer by the gate, who heard and saw it all. Thank God for this officer, because we do know how things can change when officers just believe a woman who is screaming and crying. He told the other sheriffs my story and said the same thing I was telling them. They no longer believed my wife.

She was trying so hard to get me arrested, lying that I attacked her. You see, you cannot continue to hurt and harm a child of God. The more she kept trying to lie and manipulate the cops as she manipulated me, my kids, church members, family, and friends, the more it backfired on her. She knew that black men are more likely to get arrested than any other race, so she played the victim, claiming that I hurt her and beat her up. She told our 12-year-old son that daddy beat her up. My son told my mother this as well. My mother told him no you daddy did not beat your mother up.

She was trying to make me look bad. I wasn't going to tell my kids their mom attacked Ilana and me, and in doing so, she almost harmed Ilana very badly. I told my son and the kids the truth, that their mother had lied to them. I said if I had done such a horrible act, I would have been arrested and definitely not able to leave with Ilana from the incident.

The Sheriff then said, we have called the Los Angeles Police Department (LAPD) since this incident happened outside of the courthouse. I was in disbelief, exhausted from this traumatic experience and ready to tend to my daughter.

This occurred for an hour. I was in awe that the Sheriff conducted their investigation and then said, "We cannot do nothing; LAPD will."

That was odd to me as I am still on the courthouse property. We had to wait over 30 minutes for the LAPD to arrive. During this time, my daughter was screaming, shaking, and crying for an hour due to what her mother did. She was left traumatized by this incident.

My daughter cried so long her body went limp with exhaustion, and I felt myself unraveling. At one point, while I was trying to explain the situation yet again, my stomach turned and I vomited onto the ground. I couldn't even control my body. That's how disgusted I felt. That's how overwhelmed I was.

I kept thinking, what kind of mother attacks her child in public just to win a moment? What kind of person does this and then screams victim? When LAPD arrived, they interviewed everyone again. They spoke to the gate officer again. They listened to my daughter's crying and told me to calm her down. She was screaming out of control and this time lots of time had went by. I was almost in tears wishing this was a dream.

I unbuckled her from the car seat, held her close, and rocked her. "Daddy loves you so much," I whispered into her ear. "You didn't do anything wrong. You're my big girl." She looked up at me through tears and asked, "Are you in trouble, Daddy?

Will you get arrested?" The question sliced through me. A three-year-old shouldn't even know to ask that. "No," I told her. "Daddy not in trouble."

I told Ilana I had to go talk with the nice police officers for a little longer, and I would give her a prize later for being a big girl. The police officer gave my daughter some stickers, and my daughter said thank you in a small voice, still trembling. I gave my daughter my phone so she could watch cartoons. I went back and spoke with LAPD about the incident. They went to her as well to get her side of the story.

They also went to the courthouse officer who was outside managing the gate entry. He told them the same story that he told the Sheriffs, which was my side of the story. After two hours of this nightmare my daughter had to experience, they gave me the okay to leave with my daughter. As I walked away, I heard Leslie collapse again, crying loudly, performing grief like a weapon.

This was the second time she had called the police and tried to turn my protection of our child into an accusation. Both times, she passed out on the ground, crying and screaming. I am so glad those lies and cries did not faze any of those officers. Some women lie and cry, and it does work with many police officers.

I strapped my daughter in, got into the truck, and sat for a moment before starting the engine. My hands shook on the steering wheel. My throat burned. My mind felt split in half. Then I was thinking how in the world she knew we was at the courthouse. One side trying to stay calm for my child, the other side barely holding back a breakdown.

I drove home slowly, talking softly to her, promising her a treat, promising her safety, promising her normalcy, even though I didn't know how to create it anymore. That night, after I tucked the kids in, I moved through the house like a man carrying a weight nobody could see.

My restraining order against her was pending until the court date. The next day, she filed a restraining order against me. Mind you, she came to me with attacks. Men, be careful with some of these women when you separate and go through a divorce. They will lie, manipulate the children, family members, friends, and church members. Then they want to take you for all you have when they committed adultery and broke the marriage vows, we recited.

Later at the courthouse, I saw the gate entry officer, and I told him that my separated wife said I attacked her on her restraining order. He said what, when you were here first with your daughter in a stroller, and she attacked both of you when you left the courthouse? I said exactly. Can you believe that? I asked him if I could use him as a witness, and he said yes. Here is my contact information.

Her restraining order was temporarily granted. Most of her restraining orders were false, yet the commissioner believed it and granted it without hearing my side. And how Leslie wrote the order, she had to stay 100 feet away from me.

CPS got involved, and she was not allowed to see my daughter until further notice. I took my daughter to the doctor because of the bruises. The doctor did not know what it was or where it came from.

Three weeks went by before the court date to discuss the restraining order, which is a separate case from CPS. On that date, my lawyer requested a continuance as we gathered our witnesses for her disturbing the peace at my home. She cried and passed out again when the commissioner had to grant the continuance. She was still not allowed to see my daughter.

She pleaded to the commissioner that she had not seen her daughter for 3 weeks, and this hurts her. She said her daughter needs her mother. The female commissioner had a sad, concerned expression, while the recorder, who was typing, also wore a sad expression. She had already manipulated those two. If the commissioner could, she would have granted her something, since she felt so sorry for her after she passed out and cried.

Even my lawyer saw how the courts were feeling sorry for her about this after I pointed it out. However, because CPS was involved, the commissioner could not order anything. Right after I left the courthouse, I received a call from the church secretary. I did not answer the phone because I knew she was only calling because my separated wife called the pastor and cried to them because she had not seen our daughter in 3 weeks. The church secretary texted me and said the pastor would like to talk to you.

I completely ignored them, because the spirit of discernment already told me that they only called because your separated spouse called them crying and they felt sorry for her. I was not going to allow her manipulated fake tears to get to me, and the manipulation of orders as well.

Almost a month went by, and the church never called or texted me to see how I was doing. What was going on? A check-in calls to see if I needed any support, or if I needed any food, nothing.

I did not hear from them at all, not a word. I did not receive an email with support or a mail-in card. They waited until my separated wife called them right after we left the courthouse to reach out and tell me the pastor would like to talk to you. I will not be fooled and used by church members. It is crazy how even the church supported her fully and did not even care about me. It is also crazy that it was my hard-earned money given to the church, not hers, even though we are considered one, right?

We went back to court, and now an additional three weeks have gone by. She cries out again to the commissioner, and of course, she feels sorry for her again. She ordered mandatory mediation. We tried mediation, but it didn't go anywhere.

She told them he can keep the 3 boys full-time, and she just wanted her 2 girls and for them to visit me every other weekend. I said no, and I wanted to see my daughters more, with full custody. I told the mediator that my wife is the one who had an affair with a married man. Why should my kids be moved from their house, a safe and comfortable environment where they each have their own room? This is my kid's family house. The mediator said they wanted to do what was best for the kids.

I asked her if she thinks it is best for the kids to continue their daily routine as much as possible. She said yes, I said then I will continue to homeschool Ilana and she will live with me, as this was her routine while her mother went to work. The mediator was still trying to please her and saying the same thing. All the mediator wanted was to give in to mom.

She even said, "You have the boys," and Mom agreed that it is best for the boys to be with their dad, and she will have the girls.

We weren't going anywhere. I ended the meeting. I also told her I do not feel like my youngest daughter is safe due to my wife's history of having phone sex with toys in the bed while my daughter is sleeping beside her. The mediator said that there was nothing wrong with that. So much for keeping kids safe when the law says that's okay.

Imagine if I did that in the presence of my daughter while she was in bed with me. Watching porn. Playing with myself and sending videos of me jacking off.

My uncle said the daughters should be with their mom, too. I was very upset and hurt to hear him say that. She was already staying at home with me since I work from home, and I was also homeschooling her. Then he says, "Give her one of the 2 vehicles," while I was paying both car notes.

Also, my wife was trying to get me to trade my vehicle so she could get a new one in her name only. She had been plotting; she had said this while she was having an affair. I had to cut off all communication with my family as they were destroying me.

In my mind, my wife, family, friends, and the court had failed me. It was so painful for me to go through. I do not wish this pain on anyone. It fucking hurts my soul! The mediator referred me to another doctor for my daughter, and that doctor said the bruises were fading away and could not tell what caused them.

CPS called me and said I must take her to their doctor, and they examined and questioned my daughter as well. They eventually determined no child abuse and to follow up with my doctor about those marks, as it appears to be more of a skin issue.

Between the bruises, the police, the courthouse, the screaming, and the constant threat of being painted as something I wasn't, I felt like my life had become a battlefield where the rules kept changing and the truth didn't always matter. I was still cooking, still homeschooling, still picking up the boys from school, and still trying to smile as if my life was great.

But I could feel the stress living in my body, tightening my chest, shortening my patience, stealing my sleep. Then one day, in the middle of the chaos, my daughter did something that broke me open in the gentlest way. She kept calling, "Daddy... daddy... daddy..." and without meaning to, I raised my voice, sharp from exhaustion. "What?" I snapped.

She didn't flinch. She didn't get offended. She just looked at me and said, calmly, like she knew exactly what I needed, "Daddy, I love you so much." I felt tears rush to my eyes so fast I couldn't stop them. I dropped what I was doing, knelt down, and pulled her into my arms.

"Daddy loves you so much," I whispered. "I'm sorry for getting loud." I held her until her little arms loosened around my neck. Then I turned away quickly, because I didn't want her to see the tears running down my face. But they came anyway.

Because in a season where everything felt like it was falling apart, that small sentence from a three-year-old sounded like God reminding me I still had something worth fighting for.

PART IV

REBUILDING AND REFLECTIONS

CHAPTER 16

PICKING UP
THE PIECES

The shifts didn't happen in a single revelation. It happened on the kind of morning that used to feel routine before betrayal made every routine feel haunted. The alarm went off, and for half a second, I forgot things changed. I forgot the separation, the divided house, the silence between schedules and court dates. Then I opened my eyes and remembered.

The truth hit my chest like weight. The life I built was no longer whole, and I still had to move through the day like it was. I rolled out of bed, stood in the hallway, and listened. The house was quiet except for the soft hum of the refrigerator and the occasional creak of the floor. In that quiet, I could feel how much had changed, not just in my marriage, but in me.

I walked into the kitchen and started the morning routine, lunches, water bottles, backpacks, shoes, a quick breakfast. I moved with efficiency because if I slowed down too much, the grief would catch me. The kids were half-awake, faces puffy, voices small. One of them asked something simple like where a jacket was or where a folder went and my patience snapped sharper than I meant it to. I saw their eyes widen, and I hated myself for it.

I took a breath, softened my voice, and kept going, but the damage lingered in the air. Betrayal had turned me into someone who had to manage himself in real time, constantly checking his tone, his reactions, his spirit, because the children were watching and absorbing. That's what nobody tells you, grief doesn't only live in your thoughts. It leaks into your behavior.

After drop-off, I didn't drive straight home. I pulled into a quiet side street and parked. My hands stayed on the steering wheel, tight enough to make my knuckles pale. My body was doing that familiar thing again, tight chest, shallow breathing, that restless pressure behind my ribs. I stared through the windshield like I was looking at something far away, but really, I was trying to keep myself from falling apart in public.

I whispered a prayer, not the polished kind, not the kind that sounds strong. Just the kind you say when you're trying not to break. Then my voice cracked, and I cried quietly at first, then hard, the way you cry when you've been holding it all in for too long. When the tears slowed, anger rushed in behind them. I slammed my fist into the seat once, not to damage anything, but because the pressure needed somewhere to go.

Then I went still again. That was the rhythm of my days now. I was trying to hold it together, not fall apart, pull myself back if I did. Back at the house, I walked down the hallway and saw the family photos still hanging in place, smiling versions of us frozen in time. For weeks I had walked past them like they didn't exist, like I could live alongside the lie without touching it.

But that morning, something in me finally refused. I stood in front of the first frame. One of the big ones, the kind you hang because you believe you're building something permanent. My throat tightened. I reached up, lifted it off the wall, and felt the weight of it in my hands. It wasn't heavy, but it felt heavy.

I carried it to the dining table and set it down. Then I took another. And another. One by one, I removed the images of a marriage that no longer existed, stacking them carefully like I was dismantling a shrine. The kids watched from the doorway.

My youngest, still small enough to speak the truth without understanding it fully, pointed at one of the pictures and said, "Daddy, I remember when Mommy was here." Her voice was innocent, almost nostalgic, like she was talking about a toy she couldn't find. Then she added, matter-of-fact, "I go to Mommy's house on Thursday." That sentence landed in me like grief made physical.

She was three years old and already living a split life, already learning the language of schedules and switching homes, already adjusting to a new normal she never chose. I forced myself to nod, to keep my face calm, but inside I felt something collapse. I didn't just miss my wife.

I missed my child's uninterrupted childhood. I missed being able to tuck her in every night without counting days.

That afternoon, bath time came, and it exposed another kind of loss. My youngest loved when I bathed her. She always had. She would sit in the warm water with her toys and talk to me about everything and nothing, and those little conversations were how I measured the health of our home. That day, she looked up at me with wet cheeks and said, almost pleading, that she wanted Daddy to bathe her.

I had been tired so many nights in the past. I was working multiple jobs, too tired from carrying everybody, yet I still went upstairs because she wanted me. Now, I realized how many moments I used to take for granted. I knelt by the tub, washed her hair gently, listened to her little stories, and felt the ache of knowing I wouldn't get to do this every day anymore. Betrayal didn't only take my marriage; it took my ordinary fatherhood and turned it into something scheduled, limited, and negotiated.

Later, when my older daughter's weekend visit came, the house felt briefly fuller and then immediately fragile. She arrived Friday evening, and by the time I really settled into her presence, Sunday morning was already approaching. She moved through the house like someone who belonged and didn't belong at the same time. When she woke up on Sunday, she was already preparing to leave, already pulled toward her mother's side of the divide.

I watched her pack up and felt the sting of something I couldn't control; the daughter I raised, the one I did everything for, choosing to leave quickly regardless of what had been done to our family. I had to remind myself that she was still a child, still vulnerable to influence, still shaped by the emotional gravity of the parent who played the victim best. My frustration aimed itself at the situation, not at her, but it hurt all the same. There are pains you don't get to argue with. You just have to carry them.

That night, I kissed the kids, goodnight one by one. This was a part of the routine I refused to abandon. I sat in the hallway outside their rooms and listened to their breathing. The house looked different without the pictures. The walls were bare in places, and those empty spaces felt honest. I didn't feel healed.

I didn't feel victorious. I felt tired in a deeper way, the kind of tired that lives in your bones. I also felt something else, faint but real. The sense that I was no longer just reacting to what had been done to me. I was making choices in response to it.

I was removing lies from my walls. I was protecting my peace in small, practical ways. I was learning how to stay present with my children even when my heart was split open. I used to think faith meant swallowing pain quietly and calling it strength.

But the longer I lived inside the aftermath, the more I understood that restraint is not denial, and strength is not silence. Strength is noticing when anger is trying to shape you and refusing to let it. Strength is sitting in a parked car and praying instead of spiraling. Strength is choosing therapy when pride tells you to suffer alone. Strength is admitting that betrayal changed you then deciding you will not let it turn you into someone you don't recognize.

That was the moment became real for me. So real, I could have stayed frozen in grief, but instead I stood in my own house and took the pictures down. It wasn't dramatic. It wasn't revenge. It was a quiet decision to stop worshiping what was already dead.

My wife broke vows. She broke trust. She broke the home I believed in. But that night, sitting outside my children's rooms, I realized I still had control over the man I became after it. I didn't know what the future would look like, and I still don't. But I gave myself permission to move forward one visible act at a time, not because the pain was gone, but because I refused to let the pain be the author of the rest of my life.

CHAPTER 17

FINDING STRENGTH

There's a point in every storm where the noise fades; not because the storm is over, but because you've finally gone numb. I remember sitting alone in the kitchen one night, staring at a sink full of dishes, kids asleep in their rooms, and thinking this is it. This is the life I didn't choose.

No more fake family dinners. No more Sunday greetings. No more handholding in prayer circles with people who knew more than they said and said less than they should. I was surrounded by silence, and for the first time, it didn't scare me. It told me the truth.

I had nothing left to give anyone but my children. And even then, I worried it wasn't enough.

But something strange happens when you lose everything you thought made you strong. You begin to see the strength that was quietly there all along; the kind that isn't loud or impressive, just consistent. The strength to get out of bed.

To pack lunches. To show up to work and not break in front of your coworkers. To answer your child's question without bitterness in your voice. There were nights I broke down after they went to bed, curled on the floor of my room with nothing but the sound of my own breath and a prayer I didn't know how to finish. But even in that, I kept going.

One evening, my youngest brought me a drawing; stick figures of our family, minus their mother. When I asked why she wasn't in it, she shrugged and said, "Because she doesn't live here anymore." It wasn't said with anger. Just the truth. Kids see clearly what adults try to deny.

That moment broke me, and it rebuilt me. I wasn't just surviving anymore. I was fighting to give my kids something better; not a perfect father, but a present one. Not a hero, but a man who showed them what healing looks like when everything falls apart. A friend of mine reached out to me unexpectedly.

He didn't ask for details. He didn't offer advice. He just said, "I've got time if you need to talk." I didn't realize how much I needed that until I started talking. And once I did, I couldn't stop.

He became a quiet lifeline, no judgment, no scripture quotes, and no forced forgiveness. Just a reminder that not everyone walks away. Over time, I stopped trying to fix the narrative.

I stopped trying to get people to believe me, side with me, understand the whole truth, and support me. I let go of the need to be heard by those who had already decided not to listen.

Instead, I listened to myself. I started doing small things that made me feel alive again, going to the gym, taking walks alone, reading books that didn't have answers but helped me ask better questions, and praying without trying to impress God with my pain. Just raw honesty; I'm angry, I'm hurt, and I'm still here.

There was no breakthrough moment, no dramatic transformation. Just a quiet shift. One morning, I looked in the mirror and didn't see a broken man. I saw a father, a survivor, and a truth-teller. Someone who had walked through hell and came out carrying fire in his eyes, not to burn, but to light the way forward.

I used to think strength was about not breaking. Now I know it's about breaking openly, healing honestly, and standing back up without needing to explain why. I don't have all the answers. I still have scars, but I also have clarity.

She didn't define me. They didn't destroy me. And I didn't give up; that's strength. The kind no one can take from me again.

CHAPTER 18

REDEFINING FAITH AND FAMILY

T he moment that marked the shift didn't feel dramatic at first. It happened on a quiet Sunday morning, the first time I walked into a new church after leaving the one that had once felt like home. I sat in the parking lot longer than I needed to, engine off, hands resting on the steering wheel as doubt tried to talk me into driving away.

For years, I had clung to the image of a perfect family; one marriage, five kids, united in faith and church community. That image had been everything I worked for, prayed for, and dreamed about.

I believed that if I could just keep everyone in line, hold onto traditions, and follow the rules, our family would be safe and unbreakable. Betrayal shattered that illusion in a way I never saw coming. It tore through the fabric of my life, leaving me with nothing but raw edges and questions.

But that breaking was necessary. It forced me to see that the old definitions of family, rigid, flawless, picture-perfect, were holding me hostage to expectations that no real family can live up to.

As I stepped out of the car and looked at the unfamiliar building, I realized I wasn't just visiting a new church. I was walking into a new version of my life.

The lobby buzzed with quiet conversation and the smell of coffee. No one stared. No one whispered. People simply smiled and said good morning as if I belonged there, even though they had never seen me before. I found a seat toward the middle, my kids settling beside me, and for the first time in a long while, I noticed my shoulders begin to lower. The service started on time, and within minutes I sensed something different.

There was no performance, no drawn-out rituals, no pressure to appear strong. The message was direct, grounded, and strangely personal, as if it had been written for the exact season I was living through. I caught myself leaning forward, listening in a way I hadn't for years. Somewhere between the opening prayer and the closing song, I felt something loosen inside me, a knot I didn't know I had been carrying.

When the service ended after about an hour, I didn't rush out. I sat there while people gathered their things, absorbing what had just happened.

As we walked toward the exit, I realized something else, I hadn't heard a single request for money. No extended speech about offerings, no ritualized giving moment. It confused me at first because I was so used to it.

Afterward, I approached a volunteer and asked how donations worked. She smiled and simply pointed me to a few options. No pressure. No theatrics. Just information.

I had been ready to leave my former church long before the betrayal surfaced. Even during the pandemic, when the pastor demanded in-person attendance and repeated the same messages week after week, something in my spirit had already begun to disconnect. I told my wife that year that I no longer felt the presence of God there.

Members had been quietly leaving, and now I understood why. I also saw former members at this church. Sometimes your spirit recognizes what your mind is slow to accept, when it's time to move.

Later that afternoon, I logged into the church portal, created an account, and donated. There was a section asking if I needed prayer.

I hesitated, staring at the screen longer than I expected. Then I typed the truth, I am going through a divorce and raising five kids mostly on my own. Please pray for us.

I clicked submit and closed the laptop, not expecting much to come from it. A week later, a handwritten card arrived in the mail.

I remember standing at the kitchen counter turning the envelope over in my hands. It was addressed to me by name. Inside were words of encouragement and scripture, written carefully by someone who didn't know me, yet took time out of their life to remind me that God had not forgotten me.

Then another card came. And another. Soon they were arriving once or twice a week; some typed, some handwritten, and all sincere. I would open them slowly, often after long days of cooking, cleaning, working, and parenting, when exhaustion made everything feel heavier. The timing was perfect. Every card seemed to arrive exactly when I needed it most.

I found myself wondering why strangers were showing me a level of care that many people in my own circle never had. Where were the consistent texts from family? The handwritten notes from friends? The prayers from the church I had served for years? Yet here were people who owed me nothing, reminding me that I was being lifted in prayer. Those cards didn't just encourage me, they strengthened me.

Alongside three faithful friends who were once merely acquaintances, there were also strangers at the new church who refused to let me drown. Together, they carried me through a season when I was dangerously close to giving up.

Some of the cards that carried me through that season reminded me of truths I desperately needed to hear, that God would never leave me, that His plans were still good, that I could cast my anxiety on Him because He cared. Those weren't just scriptures on paper; they became lifelines. They arrived in my mailbox, but they landed in my spirit.

Below are just some of the amazing words on the cards. Since the cards addressed me by name, they felt really personal and heartfelt.

The God who spoke the world into being, who split the Red Sea, who raised Jesus from the dead, is the same God living in every person belonging to Him. I'm praying His power works mightily in you today.

We are more than conquerors through Him who loved us. Romans 8:37 NKJV. God is love, and God's love is the best kind of love you can have in your heart. Faith can move mountains. Matthew 12:20. May you know, The Joy of His Resurrection.

The abundance of his life, the peace of his perseverance, the wonder of his love wishing you blessings today and always. Church Care Card Ministry. "Therefore, encourage one another and build each other up, just as in fact you are doing." 1 Thessalonians 5:11. Please know someone at Shepard Church is praying for you.

Heart Image. "I will never leave you nor forsake you" Hebrews 13:5 NKJV. Jesus loves you! Just wanted to let you know that someone at church is praying for you. For I know the plans I have for you declares the Lord.

Plans to prosper you and not harm you. Plans to give you hope and a future. Jeremiah 29:11. Lifting you up today with love from the Care Card Ministry. "Let love and faithfulness never leave you." Prov. 3:3

His love endures forever! Warm greetings to you. I pray this card finds you well and that every need in your life is being met. I pray that you will always be under the favor of our Lord and Savior Jesus Christ in your coming and in your going. Love, the Care Card Ministry.

"Cast all your anxiety on Him because He cares for you." 1 Peter 5:7. We are thinking of you and praying for you! It's our privilege and honor to do so, too. We lift you up today. Mark 8:31, "And He began to teach them that the son of man must suffer many things and be rejected by the elders and chief priest, scribes, and be killed, and after 3 days rise again. With love from the Care Card Ministry.

Isaiah 40:31 "But they who wait for the Lord shall renew their strength; they shall mount up with wings like eagles; they shall run and not be weary; they shall walk and not faint." Just wanted you to know that someone at church is praying for you! Lifting you up today. Care Card Ministry.

Dear, Terrance, beloved of the Lord. The Lord has appeared old to me saying: "Yes, I have loved you with an everlasting love; therefore, with loving kindness I have drawn you. Jeremiah 31:3. But now, thus says the Lord, who created you, O Jacob, and he who formed you O Israel: "Fear not, for I have redeemed you; I have called you by your name; you are mine. When you pass through the waters, I will be with you; and through the rivers, they shall not overflow you.

When you walk through the fire, you shall not be burned, nor shall the flame scorch you. Isaiah 43: 1-2. Sincerely,

"Cast all your anxiety on Him because He cares for you. 1 Peter 5:7 Valentine's greetings to you, we are thinking of you and praying for you! Bask in the love of the Lord today. 1 Peter 4:8 "Above all, keep loving one another earnestly, since love covers a multitude of sins". We lift you up today.

Dear Terrance, we wanted to let you know that you and your family are in our prayers. Our God of comfort, peace, love and grace is with you during this season of life. "May God of hope fill you with all joy and peace as you trust in him. So that you may overflow with hope by the power of the Holy Spirit". Romans 15:13. God Bless you abundantly.

One afternoon, while I was working from home, my three-year-old tugged on my sleeve and asked, "Daddy, when are you going to play with me?" I looked at my screen, then at her hopeful face, and closed the laptop. We sat on the floor building towers that kept falling over, and she laughed every single time.

In the middle of that laughter, she suddenly wrapped her arms around me and said, "Daddy, I love you so much." She didn't know it, but that sentence anchored me. I held her tightly, whispering that I loved her too, fighting back tears she was too young to understand. She has no idea how many times her small voice pulled me back from emotional cliffs. She gave me hope without trying.

That season taught me something I had never fully grasped before; faith is not performance. For years, I thought faith lived in appearances. Sunday attendance, leadership roles, traditions, and keeping the image intact.

I realized that faith is deeply personal. It is the quiet moments of doubt, the whispered prayers in the dark, the slow, stubborn hope that refuses to be crushed by disappointment. I learned that my relationship with God could survive, even thrive apart from the religious systems that had wounded me. God wasn't absent in the silence of the church pews; he was waiting in the silence of my heart, waiting for me to come home, as I was broken but willing.

Rebuilding family meant letting go of who I thought we should be and embracing who we really were. It meant creating spaces where honesty mattered more than perfection, where my kids could ask hard questions and express pain without fear. It meant surrounding myself with people who offered real compassion, not curiosity or empty advice. Parenting took on new meaning. I wasn't just teaching my children how to behave, I was teaching them how to live truthfully, how to love fiercely, how to break cycles of silence and shame.

I wanted them to know that brokenness doesn't disqualify anyone from love or belonging; it simply means we're human. This new faith is not tidy. It doesn't offer easy answers or church platitudes. It embraces mystery, struggle, and the courage to say, "I don't have it all figured out." It's a faith made stronger, not weaker, because it's tested in the fire.

And family? Family became less about bloodlines or appearances and more about commitment, living daily with grace, honesty, loyalty, and presence.

It became a living thing, not a framed photo on a wall. I will always carry scars. But I've traded illusions for truth, brokenness for authenticity, and isolation for connection.

This is my family now. This is my faith now. And this is enough.

Songs that help me through my journey include:

- "Firm Foundation." The Maverick Way Reimagined, 2024
- "Hard Fought Hallelujah." King of Hearts, 2025
- "When I Fall (Leaked Demo)." Honest Conversations, Capitol CMG Publishing, 2025
- "Nothing Else." Awe + Wonder, 2019
- "Desperate Song." Desperate, 2025"
- Here as in Heaven." Here as in Heaven, 2016
- "Lonely Dirt Road." From A Man's Perspective, 2024

Today, when I pray, my words are simpler but far more real. God is no longer just the center of the life I tried to display. He is the foundation of the life I am rebuilding. He is the reason I am still standing. I believe the enemy tests us to provoke reactions rooted in anger and despair, but I have learned to step back and let God fight the battles I cannot.

I am a follower of Jesus Christ. He is my Lord and Savior.

And though the road has been marked by betrayal and grief, I walk it now with the quiet confidence that I am not abandoned. I am held. I am guided. And somehow, through the breaking, I am becoming whole again.

CHAPTER 19

SOCIAL MEDIA SUPPORT SYSTEM

S ocial media was the new normal for me now that I didn't have many people to talk to. It seemed like every post I scrolled past was about what I was going through. When I was at my lowest, there were endless posts with scriptures that matched exactly how I was feeling. There was a day when I just couldn't stop myself from crying, and Psalm 56:8. It reads, "Tears are prayers too, they travel to God when we can't speak". God knows your pain and he knows exactly what you are going through.

When I was dealing with my ex-wife disrespecting me, it seemed like no one had anything to say except the people on social media. I came across a TikTok influencer's video saying that disrespect is closure. Even mentioning that it's exactly what I need to begin my healing journey and forgive myself. A reason to move on.

One said that you should treat them like they don't exist anymore, so that you can stop being mad. I couldn't agree more when he said that it is hard to be mad at someone you didn't know was alive. A few videos later, another TikTok user said that people would mistreat you and then try to control you. That was exactly what my ex-wife was doing. Once I started feeling like I no longer wanted to be around certain people and places, it seemed like TikTok was in my head.

How did it know to make my algorithm show me videos of people validating my emotions? It was right on time to see videos that told me things like, "It was never a loss for me. They lost a good one." They were right. There were a lot of people who made me feel I had to explain myself because I never knew if my ex-wife was saying negative things about me behind my back.

I saw a video saying, "If the level of human decency and respect is not there, then walk away respectfully. You owe them no explanation for your departure. Walk away silently and respectfully." One day, while scrolling through Facebook I saw that a friend posted a video about someone who had just gotten divorced. How ironic, considering that this friend was also friends with my ex-wife.

I figured she knew, but then I realized neither of us had spoken to her in years. But the video said verbatim the text I sent to my friend who has been supporting me throughout this time of grief. This video had a woman saying she was betrayed, gaslighted, and disrespected, while I was always genuine and pure. I guess we both won't forget this experience. As the days went by, I found myself drowning in social media. It gave me the comfort that I needed.

The advice that I longed for. Strangers who have had the same experience find each other and tell their stories. Even the comments on these videos were filled with stories. I almost wanted to add everyone as friends, like this was a support group. That's really what I wanted from my church, family, and friends, but clearly that would be asking for too much.

There was also a lot of truth in these posts, some more brutal than others. I didn't really care for the post with people telling me that I needed to let the whole situation go. Others were nice, reminding me that the best peace comes from making yourself unavailable. The worst feeling is realizing that detachment also comes with no forcing, chasing, or begging. The truth, for me, was that I could make my ex-wife do the right things.

I couldn't beg her to tell the truth or follow her to the places she went to prove my truth. I had to let her do whatever she wanted since that seemed to be her plan anyway. When I came across a post on Instagram that quoted Matthew 24:13, saying, "You're gonna make it no matter what it looks like." That's when I realized the biggest part of this entire experience. The only person you can turn to is God. The only person that can save you is God.

There is no one to go to but him. I write this book unapologetically, knowing I've been through so much heartbreak, betrayal, and disappointment. Stand alone when you feel like no one is with you. You have nothing to lose. The only thing you have to gain is the power of Jesus Christ.

The best decision I made was to be quiet. I have nothing to prove. I am not convincing anyone that I am a great person. I am not fixing what I did not break. I am not fighting for anyone to see my worth.

Whatever you do is on you. Just hope you do not regret it. As for me, I am moving forward, free and at peace. Keep betting on yourself. You are the best investment you will ever make.

Once you lose access to me, do not expect the same me you once had. Expect the version you deserve, from the energy you created. I no longer listen to what people say; I just watch what they do. Behavior never lies.

Cutting people off and letting them live with whatever delusional story suits them best is top-tier.

Pain changes people. It makes them trust less, overthink more, and shut people out. Your next chapter will make some people wish they had treated you better. The most dangerous anger comes from someone with a good heart. They hold it in, stay calm, and forgive, until one day, they can't anymore.

Don't push a good person too far. A friend of mine, whom I always vent to about everything, told me to stop apologizing for expressing myself to people I trust.

He sent me a video once that I watch weekly that says you're allowed to talk about what people did to you. The guy in the video goes on to say that it's ok to tell others how someone hurt you. He told me not to care if the person who hurt me got mad when I explained what they did, because if they wanted to keep a positive reputation, they would have treated me better.

I couldn't do anything but agree and allow myself to be ok with telling my truth. Social media reminded me to stand firm in my decisions when I cut people off and left the places that once made me feel comfortable. Seemed like no matter what platform I was on, each post provided me with posts reminding me to no longer react, argue, or get involved in drama. Why allow people who are irrelevant to keep me from protecting my peace? It's pointless.

It's also expected that these same people will feel irritated because I set boundaries. They'll think I changed, but really, I just started doing what I needed to in order to start healing, stop settling, and put myself first. Detachment was a big topic once we stopped living together. I was learning to let people be who they want to be and decide if I want them in my life. Trust that rejection is always a redirection to something bigger and better.

Redirection comes with letting go, because of how you have to grow in this moment. You have to become better than you were, and sometimes that means letting people go. Some people are meant only to help you grow, not to be in your life forever. Once I realized this, it made me think about the fact that everything could be falling apart to come together in a way I can't guess. In turn, I think the best thing social media could say is, focus only on what you can control. Let God handle the rest.

PART V

SPIRITUAL BATTLE AND HEALING

CHAPTER 20

THE SPIRIT OF DISCERNMENT

G od will give you the spirit of discernment when you choose to follow Him and trust Him. I prayed and prayed to God to please remove anyone from my life who should not be there. Remove all those who are trying to harm me, who are trying to destroy my family, who do not want to see me happy, and remove all the jealous souls, including family members and friends. God said no weapon form against me shall prosper.

Years ago, when I was living in another state, my dad told me that my brother is very jealous and envious of me. I wish he had never told me that. I was so hurt.

He shared with me other things, but I couldn't understand why he was so envious and jealous of me. I never did anything to him. I brag about him all the time to people saying how well he is doing. However, I was not surprised because the signs were always there, I just chose to ignore them and accepted him for who he was.

The "spirit of discernment" refers to a heightened ability to make wise judgments and distinguish between right and wrong, often in a spiritual or moral context. It involves careful consideration, insightful analysis, and the ability to differentiate between truth and deception, or good and evil. This discernment can be seen as a gift, a skill, or a trait that enables individuals to navigate complex situations and make informed decisions. Here's a more detailed explanation:

1. Spiritual Discernment:

- In a religious context, discernment is often understood as the ability to identify the true nature of spiritual influences, distinguishing between the work of the Holy Spirit, good influences, and evil influences such as demonic deception.
- It involves a deep understanding of God's character and the teachings of the faith, allowing individuals to discern truth from error and make choices that align with God's will.
- It is a gift that helps individuals to see through deceptive schemes and make decisions that reflect God's wisdom and guidance.
- Discernment is often associated with the ability to recognize false prophets, false teachings, and deceptive spirits.
- It is cultivated through prayer, study of scripture, and reliance on the Holy Spirit.

2. Practical Discernment:

- Discernment can also be applied to everyday life, enabling individuals to make wise decisions in various situations.
- It involves careful consideration of options, weighing the evidence, and making choices based on sound reasoning and understanding.

- It can involve evaluating character, judging motives, and understanding the underlying influences behind someone's actions.
- Discernment in practical matters can help individuals avoid mistakes, make sound financial decisions, and navigate interpersonal relationships with greater clarity and wisdom.

3. Developing Discernment:

- Discernment is often seen as a skill that can be developed through practice and a willingness to learn.
- It requires a commitment to seeking the truth, being open to new perspectives, and examining one's own biases and assumptions.
- Prayerful reflection, seeking guidance from trusted mentors, and studying the Word of God are all avenues for cultivating discernment.
- Discernment is not about making snap judgments, but about careful consideration and a willingness to seek the truth.

In essence, the "Spirit of discernment" is about having the wisdom and insight to make wise judgments, especially in matters of spiritual and moral significance. It involves a combination of spiritual awareness, practical judgment, and a commitment to seeking truth and understanding.

Paul the Apostle mentions the gift of discerning spirits in 1 Corinthians 12:10. John Chrysostom, in his interpretation of this passage, says that these words mean the ability to tell who is spiritual and who is not, who is a prophet and who is not, as Paul wrote at the time of many false prophets.

I see so many fake family members, church members, and friends. They will publicly pray for a celebrity stranger, but not for a hurting family member on the phone or through a text message. I saw this with my own eyes. Shockingly, the first person to pray for me was a real estate agent I had never spoken to in years. She immediately stopped what she was doing, moved away from her kids, and just prayed. Later, my grandmother prayed for me on the phone, although she wanted to pray for forgiveness and take my ex back. That is when I told her not to pray that prayer to take her back, because that is not what I am praying for, and she laughed.

CHAPTER 21

SPIRITUAL WARFARE

S piritual warfare is a deeply personal and often intense struggle. It is the invisible battle between forces of good and evil; often seen as a conflict between one's spiritual growth or peace and the things (internal or external) that seek to hinder it. For a long time, I thought the greatest fight of my life was saving my marriage. I was wrong. The greatest fight was learning how to survive after it ended without losing my faith, my identity, or my soul.

There came a quiet evening when I realized something inside me had shifted. The house was still. The children were asleep. I sat alone at the kitchen table, the same table where we once planned vacations, discussed our dreams, and laughed about the future. Now it held only silence.

In that silence, I understood that I could not keep living as if my healing depended on what she did next, what others believed, or whether justice would ever look the way I imagined. Something in me released that night. Not all at once, but enough for me to breathe differently.

You cannot just go to the altar for prayer and then do what you want to people and expect God to answer all your prayers. Then people have been fooled by pastors and others by telling them God forgives you, and in the name of Jesus, you are healed and saved immediately, then they move on to continue to hurt others and then keep saying God forgive me.

That is not how healing works. There are consequences for harming others, especially when those harms are deliberate. Time alone does not correct what the heart refuses to confront. The idea that "time heals all pain" is comforting, but only partly true. Time creates distance, but what you do within that distance determines whether you heal or remain stuck inside the wound.

I learned that healing is active. It requires surrender, honesty, and courage.

What Time Can Do:

- Soften intensity: Over time, most emotional pain becomes less sharp. The initial shock or grief can fade.
- Offer perspective: With distance, people often understand events differently, sometimes finding meaning or learning from them.
- Create space for growth: As life moves on, new experiences can bring joy, purpose, or connection again.

What Time Can't Do Alone:

- Erase deep wounds: Some traumas, losses, or regrets may never fully disappear without intentional healing.
- Replace processing: Unprocessed grief, guilt, or trauma can linger, even years later.

- Act as a substitute for support: Therapy, connection with others, or self-reflection often play a crucial role.

Time can help, but often, what we do with time matters more than time itself.

Whether you view spiritual warfare through a religious lens (e.g., Christianity, Islam, etc.) or as a metaphor for inner conflict, here's a grounded breakdown:

What Is Spiritual Warfare?

In many traditions, spiritual warfare includes:

- Temptation and doubt
- Despair, fear, or oppression
- Conflict with negative forces (internal or external)
- Battles over purpose, identity, and faith

Signs You Might Be in Spiritual Warfare

- Persistent negative thoughts or emotional heaviness
- Feeling distant from your faith or purpose
- Internal battles with guilt, shame, or hopelessness
- Recurring destructive behaviors or patterns

How to Respond to Spiritual Warfare?

1. Spiritual Disciplines

- Prayer: Regular, honest connection with the divine. Ask for strength and discernment.
- Scripture/Spiritual reading: Use sacred texts to anchor truth and encouragement.

- Fasting or Meditation: Helps clear mental and spiritual space for clarity.

2. Guard Your Mind

- Recognize and reject thoughts that are deceptive, accusatory, or shaming.
- Replace them with affirmations rooted in love, faith, or spiritual truth.

3. Community Support

- Don't isolate yourself. Share with trusted spiritual mentors, friends, or counselors.
- Collective prayer, worship, or conversation can strengthen resolve and give perspective.

4. Live Intentionally

- Align your daily actions with your values and faith.
- Do good even when you don't feel good — action often leads the soul.

5. Spiritual Armor (from Ephesians 6:10–18).

- Truth, righteousness, peace, faith, salvation, and the Word. These are described as your protection.
- This metaphor encourages being equipped and vigilant.

Spiritual warfare isn't always dramatic; it can be silent and slow. But you're not alone in it. Whether you see this as a test of faith, a psychological challenge, or a mixture of both, facing it with purpose, support, and truth can bring strength and peace.

Depression isn't just sadness; it can feel like:

- Emptiness or numbness
- Lack of motivation, even for things you used to enjoy

- Overwhelming fatigue or mental fog
- Isolation, even when surrounded by others
- Harsh self-judgment or thoughts like "What's the point?"

What's Actually Happening?

Depression often involves both emotional and biological components:

- Neurochemical changes (like serotonin or dopamine imbalances)
- Cognitive distortions: your mind starts telling you lies that feel true
- Life events or trauma can trigger or deepen it
- Sometimes, no clear reason and that's okay too. It's still real.

What Helps: Even If It Feels Impossible

1. Speak to Someone (Please Don't Do It Alone)

- A therapist, doctor, or mental health counselor can help more than you may expect.
- If you're spiritual, a trusted mentor or faith leader can also offer support.
- Even a friend who listens without judgment can be a light in the dark.

2. Tiny Acts of Self-Care

- Forget perfection. Focus on small, manageable things:
  - Drink water
  - Step outside for 5 minutes
  - Write a few words about what you're feeling (no pressure to be eloquent)
  - Take a shower, even if it feels like a mountain

3. Name the Lies

- Depression often whispers things like:
    - "You're worthless."
    - "You'll never get better."
    - "No one would miss you."
    - These are lies. Name them. Challenge them. You don't have to believe everything you think when you're hurting.

4. Structure Helps

Even minimal routines (wake up, get dressed, move, eat something) create a rhythm that can help rewire your mental state over time.

5. Medication Can Be Life-Changing (and There's No Shame)

Sometimes, depression is too deep for willpower or lifestyle changes alone. If it's an option for you, talk to a doctor about treatment.

You're Not Weak. You're Fighting.

If you're reading this, you're still here, and that matters. You may not feel hope, but I'll hold onto it for you if you need me to.

A Prayer for When You're Struggling with Depression

God, I don't have the words.
I'm tired. I feel lost, numb, or just gone.
But here I am, even if all I can offer is silence or tears.
Please meet me in this darkness.
Hold me when I can't hold myself.
Remind me that this pain won't last forever,
even if it feels like it will.

I'm asking for peace, even a small drop.
I'm asking for strength, just enough to make it through today.
I'm asking for hope, even if I can't feel it yet.
Show me that I'm not alone.
Send someone, something, or a sign that I still matter.
Help me believe there's a purpose in my pain,
and that healing, though slow, is possible.
Thank you for staying, even when I push away.
I trust, even if barely, that you hear me. Amen.

A Christian Prayer for Depression and Emotional Pain

Heavenly Father,
I come to You broken, tired, and unsure of how to keep going.
I feel weighed down, Lord — like joy is far from me.
But I know You are close to the brokenhearted,
and You save those who are crushed in spirit (Psalm 34:18).
Even when I can't feel You, I believe You are near.
When my thoughts are dark, remind me that nothing can separate
me from Your love (Romans 8:38–39).
God, be my strength today.

Be the light in this darkness,
and the calm in my storm.
Lift my eyes when I can't lift my head.
Jesus, You knew sorrow. You wept. You suffered.
So You understand mine.

Help me to trust that You are working, even in this.
Replace these lies with Your truth:
That I am loved.
That I am chosen.
That I have a purpose.
Help me hold on when I feel like letting go.
I know You are not finished with me yet (Philippians 1:6).
Thank You for staying with me.
Even in the silence.
Even in the pain.
In Jesus' name, Amen.

📖 Verses You Can Hold Onto

❊ "The Lord is close to the brokenhearted and saves those who are crushed in spirit." – Psalm 34:18
❊ "Cast all your anxiety on Him because He cares for you." – 1 Peter 5:7
❊ "Even though I walk through the darkest valley, I will fear no evil, for You are with me." – Psalm 23:4
❊ "My grace is sufficient for you, for My power is made perfect in weakness." – 2 Corinthians 12:9

A Prayer for Healing After Infidelity

Father God,

My heart is shattered. I never imagined this kind of pain.

I feel betrayed, abandoned, and crushed by the one I loved and trusted.

Lord, I don't know what to do with this anger, this sadness, this storm.

But You are the God who binds up the brokenhearted (Psalm 147:3).

Bind me now. Hold what I can't hold.

Help me resist the lies:

That I'm not enough.

That I'll never trust again.

That I deserved this.

Heal what only You can heal, deep in my soul.

Teach me how to forgive, not to excuse, but to free myself from bitterness.

Give me wisdom, Lord, for what comes next.

Show me whether to rebuild or release.

And if I have failed You or her in any way, show me gently, but don't let shame take root.

Restore me. Renew me.

Help me believe that joy, trust, and love are still possible.

In Jesus' name, Amen.

Steps Toward Healing

1. Acknowledge Your Emotions — All of Them

Let yourself feel the rage, sorrow, disbelief. God can handle your anger and your questions. You don't have to "clean it up" for Him.

2. Seek Support

You do not have to carry this pain alone. A Christian counselor or trusted pastor can walk with you through the grief, forgiveness process, and decisions ahead.

3. Don't Rush Forgiveness or Reconciliation

Forgiveness doesn't mean trusting again immediately. And reconciliation isn't always the right outcome. Take the time you need. Ask God for wisdom (James 1:5).

4. Guard Your Heart Without Closing It

After betrayal, it's tempting to shut down emotionally; to say, "Never again." But healing means learning to love and trust again, even if it's slow.

5. Give Yourself Permission to Grieve

You're grieving more than a person; you're grieving what you thought you had, and what was lost. That grief deserves space.

Scripture to Hold Onto

* Psalm 147:3 – "He heals the brokenhearted and binds up their wounds."
* Isaiah 41:10 – "Do not fear, for I am with you... I will strengthen you and help you."
* Romans 8:28 – "And we know that in all things God works for the good of those who love Him..."
* Psalm 34:18 – "The Lord is close to the brokenhearted and saves those who are crushed in spirit."

Letting go of a relationship, especially a marriage, after betrayal is one of the hardest and bravest choices a person can make. It's not a failure. It's an act of self-respect and, often, spiritual survival. Releasing someone who broke your trust is not about bitterness; it's about protecting your peace, honoring your worth, and allowing God to lead you into healing and freedom.

Here's a Christian prayer and a release declaration to help you begin that process. Take your time with these. Let your heart feel them.

 A Prayer to Release a Relationship After Betrayal

Father,

This hurts more than I know how to say.

I gave my heart, my life, and my trust, and it was broken.

I wanted restoration, but I can't carry this pain any longer.

I release this relationship to You.

I choose not to hold onto what cannot be rebuilt.

I choose peace over resentment.

I choose healing over bitterness.

I choose to walk forward, even if I don't know where the path leads.

Lord, help me forgive, not to forget or excuse

but to untangle my soul from the weight of betrayal.

Heal me from the lies I believed in this relationship:

That I was unlovable.

That I was not enough.

That I was the reason for her choices.

I declare the truth: I am loved. I am chosen. I am Yours.

I trust that You have more for me than what I've lost.

Thank You for walking with me through this release.

Don't let my heart grow hard.
Teach me to hope again.
In Jesus' name,
Amen.

Declaration: Releasing Her, Reclaiming Yourself

You can speak this aloud or write it in a journal as a turning point moment:

Today, I release what is no longer mine to carry.
I let go of the woman who broke my trust.
I do not carry her choices or sins on my back anymore.
I forgive, not because they deserve it, but because I deserve peace.
I am no longer bound to what hurt me. I am free to heal.
I bless them, but I walk away.
I choose life, healing, and the future God has for me.
This chapter ends, but my story continues, and it is not over.

Scripture to Anchor You

* Isaiah 43:18–19 – "Forget the former things; do not dwell on the past. See, I am doing a new thing!"
* 2 Corinthians 5:17 – "If anyone is in Christ, he is a new creation; the old has gone, the new is here!"

❄ Psalm 30:5 – "Weeping may endure for a night, but joy comes in the morning."

❄ Proverbs 4:23 – "Above all else, guard your heart, for everything you do flows from it."

Letting go doesn't mean the pain stops instantly. But it does mean you're choosing to stop bleeding for someone who won't bandage the wound. You're honoring the dignity God placed inside you.

CHAPTER 22

STEPS TOWARD HEALING

Healing after a divorce is a deeply personal journey, but there are common steps that many people find helpful. These steps focus on emotional recovery, rebuilding self-identity, and moving forward with purpose.

1. Allow Yourself to Grieve

Divorce is a major loss, even if it was the right choice. Grieving is not a weakness; it's necessary.

- Accept your feelings: sadness, anger, relief, confusion—they're all normal.
- Avoid suppressing emotions: journaling or talking with someone you trust can help.

- Be patient with the process: healing isn't linear.

2. Establish Emotional Support

You don't have to go through this alone.

- Reach out to friends or family who are nonjudgmental and compassionate.
- Consider a therapist who specializes in relationships or trauma.
- Join a support group for divorced individuals (online or in-person).

3. Create Healthy Boundaries

Rebuild your life by setting new rules for interaction with your ex, especially if children are involved.

- Limit unnecessary contact.
- Communicate respectfully and clearly.
- Use tools like co-parenting apps if needed.

4. Reclaim Your Identity

After being part of a couple, it can be hard to remember who you are on your own.

- Reconnect with interests, hobbies, and values you may have set aside.
- Try new experiences to rediscover what excites or fulfills you.
- Reflect on who you are now—and who you want to become.

5. Focus on Self-Care

Your physical and mental health need attention now more than ever.

- Eat well, move your body, and prioritize sleep.
- Practice mindfulness, meditation, or prayer if helpful.
- Avoid numbing (e.g., overuse of alcohol, dating apps, etc.).

6. Redefine Your Goals and Future

Your vision of the future may have changed and it's okay to start fresh.

- Set small, manageable goals.
- Explore new career, financial, or living options if relevant.
- Begin to dream again, even if it feels distant or uncertain.

7. Forgive When You're Ready

Forgiveness is for your peace, not theirs.

- This might mean forgiving your ex, yourself, or the situation.
- You don't have to forget or justify harm, but releasing bitterness can lighten your burden.

8. Open Yourself to Growth

Divorce is painful, but it can also be transformative.

- What have you learned about yourself?
- How can this experience deepen your empathy, strength, or clarity?
- You're not broken, just changing.

Have you ever been betrayed before by others? What would you do if you were betrayed by Christians? Have you ever sought revenge on someone who betrayed you? Have you experienced a happy family fall apart?

If your answer is yes to any of the questions, please remember to always put God first in your decision, cause things can turn out very differently if you do not.

Please continue to keep on in faith and know that the devil knows exactly when to keep pressing your buttons to steer you into the dark; do not allow him to do that to you. Jesus Himself said, 'In this world you will have trouble. But take heart! I have overcome the world.' John

16:33. So even though it feels like you are carrying a heavy load, know that Jesus has already overcome the challenges we face, and He will give you the strength to endure.

Beware of your awareness of energy. Look at what drains you and what uplifts you. Remember, no one deserves full access to you. Select what you allow in your space to ensure you have peace.

- God I am worthy!
- God I am a creator!
- God will create and open doors for me!
- I am trustworthy!
- I am enough!
- I am a good father!
- I matter!
- My mental health matters!
- I will not tolerate disrespect!
- I will remove myself from toxic people,
- Let go of toxic attachments.
- Do not let people lower your energy.
- Surround yourself with positive people.
- Surround yourself with spiritual people.
- Surround yourself with people who support you with actions.
- Surround yourself with people who will actually pray with you and for you, on the phone or in person.
- I can control my emotions!
- I will not allow others to control my emotions.
- I am powerful!
- I am not broke. I am rich, says the Lord.
- I need God, I cannot fight my battles alone.
- I cannot go through life without God.
- I need you God to order my steps in your word.
- I do not need to react to others.

- I can remain silent to protect my peace.
- God remove those folks around me who have negative energy.

I have distanced myself from my family and live a peaceful life. I do not want to inform them or share anything personal with them. This was very difficult, as I was always an outgoing person who enjoyed family time. However, I must protect my peace and not let anyone disturb my mental state. I do not want to hear anything negative about another family member and gossip about them without trying to support them.

I am happy with being alone with God on my side, along with having a very, very short circle of friends whom I can count on. The sad part is that these people are not even my family, and I trust them, and they support and trust me. I had a pastor who told me when I was in high school that some people will come into your life for a reason and for a season, and you need to distinguish which one they are in.

I am preparing to write my will. When I die, please do not cry for me and send any flowers. I did not receive any flowers when I was alive; do not send any when I die. I do not want a funeral at all.

If my kids want to see me before I go six feet under, then they are the only ones who can see me with an open casket.

I've lived an intense life, and writing this book became my therapy, my peace in letting go and my reminder that only God brought me out of hell. It was God who covered me with his blood. I would like to leave you all with a prayer.

Father God, I thank you for this day. Please do not lead me into temptation, but always deliver me from evil. God, please bless me with the spirit of discernment to distinguish who is really meant to be in my life. Please break every curse against me, and do not let any weapon formed against me prosper. Continue to fight the battles I do not see and continue to pour out your blessings on me. I know I am not perfect, God, but help me live my life peacefully.

I continue to trust in God with all my heart. I pray constantly for peace and for those who are not for me, for God to remove them from my life. I pray for the blessings of God, health, wealth, and prosperity. To protect my peace, I had to cut off those family, friends, and church members who betrayed or failed to support me. I stand here unapologetic, knowing that it was by God's grace and mercy that I am still here today.

He saved my soul, healed my soul, and brought me peace. He allowed me to go through a dark place where all I could do was depend on Him and trust Him through the process. It was very difficult to trust God through the process. As a man, sometimes we want someone to pray with us, hug us, tell us it's okay to not be okay, and pray with us. We need someone to check in on us regularly and make sure we are okay. We want someone to send nice messages. We want to feel love, value, and appreciated.

CONCLUSION

B etrayal changes the shape of a life. It redraws what feels safe, what feels true, and what feels possible. Even after the facts are known and the decisions are made, the impact of betrayal often lingers in ways that are difficult to explain. Healing is not a moment of closure. It is a process of learning how to live honestly after trust has been broken.

I once believed healing meant returning to who I was before. I have learned that it means becoming someone new. The person I am now carries greater awareness, clearer boundaries, and a deeper understanding of self. Loss was part of that transformation, but so was growth.

Faith also changed. It became quieter, less performative, and more honest. I no longer measure faith by certainty or outward strength. I measure it by endurance and by the willingness to remain open even after disappointment. Faith does not always remove pain, but it can give us the strength to walk through it.

Healing required more than time. It required truth, support, and the courage to face emotions I had long avoided. It required acknowledging the psychological and emotional effects of betrayal without minimizing them. Most importantly, it required choosing to value my own well-being, even when doing so felt uncomfortable.

If you are reading this and feel exhausted, confused, or unsure of what comes next, I want you to know that your experience makes sense. You are not weak because you are struggling. You are responding to something that mattered deeply to you. Healing is not linear, and it does not require you to have everything figured out.

You do not need to rush forgiveness, force faith, or pretend you are okay when you are not. You are allowed to move at your own pace. You are allowed to set boundaries. You are allowed to grieve what was lost and still believe that something meaningful can emerge from the pain.

Betrayal does not get to define the rest of your life. It may shape you, but it does not own you. What you choose moving forward matters more than what was done to you.

Healing forward means choosing honesty over denial, boundaries over fear, and growth over resentment. It means allowing faith, however fragile, to exist without forcing it to be perfect. It means reclaiming your voice, your worth, and your future.

Wherever you are in your journey, keep going. Healing is possible. You are not alone. And your story is still being written.

A Closing Prayer

God, for those who are carrying the weight of betrayal, pain, and unanswered questions, I pray for comfort, clarity, and peace. Meet them in the places that feel broken and uncertain. Grant them strength for each step forward, wisdom to set healthy boundaries, and patience with themselves as healing unfolds. Restore what has been shaken, soften what has been hardened by hurt, and remind them that they are not forgotten, not alone, and not beyond hope. Amen.

The Journey Still Continues....

- **My Healing Journey**
- **Loving Myself First**
- **Forgiveness for Me**
- **Being at Peace**
- **God's Elevation (Major Success)**

ABOUT THE AUTHOR

Dr. Marcus Anderson is a single father of five kids who he loves so much and advocate for emotional and spiritual healing. Through lived experience and personal recovery, he writes to support those navigating betrayal, trauma, and faith reconstruction. He will continue to write as writing became his new therapy to lived experiences. Remember to keep God first and God loves you.

www.ingramcontent.com/pod-product-compliance
Lightning Source LLC
Chambersburg PA
CBHW020627110726
47899CB00002B/686